DORMITORIES, FAGS AND STICKY WILLIES

Lawrie Stone

MINERVA PRESS
LONDON
ATLANTA MONTREUX SYDNEY

DORMITORIES, FAGS AND STICKY WILLIES

ISBN 0 75410 321 8

First Published 1998 by
MINERVA PRESS
195 Knightsbridge
London SW7 1RE

Printed in Great Britain for Minerva Press

DORMITORIES, FAGS AND STICKY WILLIES

To
Kathy & Vic
with all my love
and thanks for
your encouragement
Kathy –
[illegible]
x

For my family and friends

About the Author

Lawrie Stone was born in London in 1961. Her father was a writer and poet; her mother an art school model. Together they lived the most bohemian lifestyle possible in a prefab in Clapham. In 1992 Lawrie trained as a journalist and broadcaster and has written for local and national newspapers and magazines. She is married with three children.

Contents

Dormitories, Fags and Sticky Willies 9

Cry War 39

Window Pains 53

Have You Seen the News, Mummy? 69

Sea Views 73

The Competition 89

Dormitories, Fags and Sticky Willies

'You went to boarding school!' screeched the girl in the red suit, as she surreptitiously stole the last After Eight from the plate on the table.

Clair surveyed the situation. Four of her closest friends sat around the restaurant table. She had known them for years and yet here they were, totally unaware of her past.

'How do you think I got into this habit?' she asked casually, waving her cigarette in the air and sending a waft of blue smoke up to the ceiling. Helen looked down at her suit. Clair always did that to her, managed to knock her confidence; didn't she know she only wanted to be part of her world? Did she not know she had only bought the suit because she knew she'd like it? For Christ's sake, didn't she know she was in love with her?

Clair suppressed a smile. A waiter with a hard-on refilled their glasses and left them to it. He'd seen this a hundred times before. Girls' night out, boys' night in with the children. His feet and his cock ached and he wanted to go home.

The girls hadn't noticed. They were looking at Clair now – expectant, knowing, demanding. Clair took a deep breath and began.

*

The red Mini Clubman sped along the country roads at the speed of light. The back seats were flat. Cushions that had started life as barriers to protect the children's heads were now being used to beat them in. Five girls of varying ages sat in the back. The eldest, sitting squashed against the back doors with her knees tucked up to her chin and a look of utter despair on her face was a thirteen-year-old Clair.

'How long until we get there?' she whined to her mother.

Carol wasn't listening. With one hand gripping the steering wheel she used the other to open the glove compartment. Once inside she scrabbled blindly among the empty packets of cigarettes until she found one that sounded as if it might have something in it.

'We'll get there when we bloody get there,' she hollered.

Clair looked out of the window. They were passing through the country village that led to the cottage her parents escaped to when things became too much in London. Clair recognised the fish and chip shop on the corner and knew they were nearly there.

Damned if I'm going to tell them, she thought, glaring at two of her sisters, Emma and Georgia.

Suddenly, something caught her eye. She had seen this before on these trips. A group of schoolgirls were walking down a hill as her mother screeched to a halt at the traffic lights. They were wearing long green cloaks with hoods. The linings in the hoods were different colours for different girls. Two had red. Two had yellow, but three had purple. Clair wanted one. And what she wanted, she decided she was going to get.

The house looked pretty much as they had left it the last time they visited. Set in Kent, it was a hop-picker's cottage that had long since been sold on to 'the townies', as people like Clair's parents had become known.

Inside, the walls had been covered with chip paper and painted a fashionable white. The large kitchen contained a reasonable amount of fitted units, finished off with a round table and six matching chairs, next to which stood a high chair for the baby. Above the table hung a Coca-Cola lampshade in red and white. A cup of congealed coffee on the draining board was the only sign of the last hurried exit back to London.

Clair carried her sleeping baby sister up to one of the bedrooms and laid her on the bed. The green cloaks swam back into her mind and she decided the best time to tackle the subject would be over dinner that evening.

Clair's father arrived at the cottage by seven in the evening. It had been a boiling hot day in the summer of '76, and although it was now cooler, David was walking slowly up the path that led to the back door of the cottage. Clair watched him from her bedroom window. His pinstripe suit, although expensive, now looked creased from the long drive down. His shirt was sticking to his back and the jacket of his suit hung soberly over his shoulder.

Big Alf, who both lived next door and tended to the cottage garden, was digging round a large plot of rhubarb when he saw David arrive.

'Hello there, David,' he called with a cheery wave. Digging his fork into the parched earth, Big Alf started towards his prey.

David had seen him first. Dropping his briefcase on to the parched footpath he met him halfway across the allotment.

'Hot day again,' said Big Alf, lifting his cap and wiping a sweaty brow with the back of his hand.

'Certainly is,' said Clair's father, squinting up at the last of the sun that was slowly making its way to the horizon.

'That rhubarb's coming along famously, y'know,' Big Alf was saying as Clair, who was still watching from the window, saw his son, a taller lankier version of his father, take one huge stride over the fence that separated the two properties.

Clair's mother called the son Little Alf and Alf Big Alf. This confused Clair and she decided to go downstairs and rescue her father from the clutches of the two boring Alfs.

'Mum says, can you come and carve the meat,' she called from the back door.

This was always a good way of getting her father to come into the house. Picking up his briefcase, David apologised to the two Alfs, who were looking totally rejected. They both scratched their heads at the same time, for good measure.

Once inside, David put a gentle arm around his daughter's shoulder.

'Did you think I needed rescuing, darling?' he said, and laughed.

Dinner was a noisy affair. Clair and her sister Emma mostly argued about what to watch on television that night, with Clair arguing ferociously for the merits of *Top of the Pops* while Emma fought just as hard for the continuation episode of *The Six Million Dollar Man*. All was resolved when David intervened, telling them that nobody would be watching the bloody telly tonight.

Clair's plans for a spell at boarding school were not going too well. There had been a big argument. The subject of a new school would need tackling very carefully. She decided to come straight out with it.

'Mum, Dad. You know that school up the road,' she began.

'Yes?' said both her parents together.

'Do you think perhaps I could go there one day?'

Two weeks and very little persuasion later, Clair and her mother were back home and in the school uniform shop in Bromley. Clair had been surprised at how little argument it had taken to persuade her parents to let her go; it was almost as if they'd had the same idea as her. But she decided to keep quiet about the whys and wherefores and thank her lucky stars that she was going at all.

Clair was trying on a blazer. It was green with a matching pocket that was plain in design. The woman in the shop, a bossy type with a mammoth bosom, explained that 'One had to sew the school badge on oneself.'

This only succeeded in starting Carol off. She staggered over to the sock counter and pretended to blow her nose furiously; Clair as usual stepped into the breech and told the heaving bosom that she would manage to do that herself if she could find the right colour of green cotton.

With Carol having recovered sufficiently from the giggles, the next part of the show was about to take place. It was the part that Clair had been waiting for – the part where she tried on the magical green cloak.

The assistant went over to the rack to fetch it. Here it comes, thought Clair, here it comes. It's getting closer, it's nearly here. *Got it!* The heaving bosom jumped out of her skin as Clair snatched the cloak from her.

'Well, really,' she exclaimed, 'boarding school will certainly knock the spirit out of you!'

*

The school trunk was large and green and labour-intensive. It had shiny silver studs all the way round its lid and a large silver lock with two keys. The inside was beginning to be filled with all kinds of paraphernalia. Carol was holding a list sent from the school which explained in gentle terms what uniform was needed: 'Two grey skirts to be no shorter than two inches from the floor when kneeling down,' said Carol in an unfamiliar matronly voice.

The pair of them collapsed into fits of giggles as they remembered the heaving bosom easing her cumbersome frame on to the floor of the school uniform shop and measuring earnestly the required two inches from hessian carpet to Clair's knobbly knee.

'Two sky blue jumpers,' continued Carol.

'Check,' said Clair.

'Six pairs of grey knee-high socks,' was Carol's response, followed by more hysterical laughter.

'Check!' squealed Clair, placing the neatly rolled-up socks into the trunk next to the jumpers.

'One Sunday best suit,' Carol said, 'to be worn to church on Sundays only.'

The suit in all its glory was put into the trunk.

'And finally,' said Carol, 'one hot-water bottle.'

Clair was having none of this. 'What do I need a bloody hot-water bottle for?' she said indignantly.

Carol lit a cigarette and wondered idly if she even had one in the house. 'I can get you one at Boots, darling,' she said.

With the trunk finally packed and filled with everything on the school list, apart from the offending hot-water bottle, there remained only one thing left to organise: the tuck-box. This was to contain sweets and chocolate to be eaten during recreational hours, and was a necessary requirement to boarding school life. Carol gave Clair a pound note which she was to use to buy the tuck and Clair duly trotted off to her local corner shop with the sacred whole pound to oblige.

Clair walked the familiar trail through the back streets of Bromley that led to the corner shop. She walked swiftly past old Mrs Smith, who would not only talk to her about the weather for what seemed to Clair to be ages and ages, but had the irritating habit of asking her to buy something for her. She did not even trust her with the money, and usually insisted that she keep some item Clair had on her person until she returned. On the last occasion she had insisted on holding on to her bicycle, something that had irritated the young girl intensely. Gaining speed, Clair broke into a trot and passed the old lady without eye contact and only a, 'Hi, Mrs Smith,' to keep her company on this day. It was far too an important day to be dealing with her, and within twenty paces she had reached the safety of the shop door.

A regular visitor there, she was able to browse at her leisure without being watched by the beady-eyed shop-keeper, who was continuously on the lookout for what he called 'pinchers'. This was his term for the schoolchildren who came into the shop to steal crisps or copies of *Jackie* or the *Beano*, depending on their ages and inclinations.

Clair was exempt from this tight scrutiny. This did not imply a want of trying, for Clair had many times and for many different reasons mulled over the possibilities of taking a packet of crisps or an extra jubbly, if the weather was hot, without paying.

Fortunately, through sheer determination and a perpetual fear of getting caught, she had always managed to avert her gaze from the goody filled shelves, and take only the things she could pay for. She'd never forgotten an incident when she was six years old and had eaten a strawberry from outside a greengrocer's and got caught. She always managed to go crimson with deep embarrassment afterwards whenever the assistant who'd caught her nicknamed her 'Strawberry'.

On this occasion, however, she felt that she could buy anything she desired because she had a pound. A smooth, crisp pound note that was to be spent just on her; not only was it to be used exclusively for sweets, but for once in her life they did not have to be shared with her sisters. Things were most definitely looking up for Clair!

The shopkeeper was a man in his early sixties. Small and thin, he wore his glasses propped on the end of an angular nose, accentuating his eyes and adding to the po-faced reputation he had among the locals who used the store and the children who frequented it, often with a shoplifting intent. At sixty-five Bob Reeves was near to retirement age and looking forward to it.

The thieving that took place at school kicking-out time drove him crazy. He was on medication for acid stomach bought on by stress and his wife nagged at him to sell the shop constantly. He was fed up with her demands for a cottage in the country with roses over the door, and although sick to death of 'the pinchers', he felt an affinity with the old shop that kept him at his place behind the till.

Now, here was young Clair Hollands, he said to himself, and she's breezing into the shop without a care in the world, umming and ah-ing over the sweet counters.

'How much are these, Mr Reeves?' she asked.

'Let me see now,' replied the old man. 'Twenty packets of chewing gum – that will be one pound exactly.'

When Clair got home with the chewing gum, Carol hit the roof.

'Clair, what on earth possessed you? What makes you think that you can start at a new school with all those packets of chewing gum? What made you buy all that chewing gum?'

The questions kept coming, the anger became apparent and Clair hated her for spoiling a precious and carefree half-hour spending on something she knew was not allowed. Bugger! she thought – an expletive she had learned from her grandfather. Bugger that, and bugger the chewing gum! With no suitable explanation forthcoming for her mother she ran to her room, slammed the door and kicked the school trunk just for good measure before collapsing on to the bed in floods of tears.

What would the Famous Five do? she wondered. Surely her mother realised that was what boarding school was all about… midnight feasts of cakes and forbidden chewing gum, pillow fights and secrets shared between girls. Defeated, she picked up Enid Blyton's *Second Form at Malory Towers* and started to read.

Carol in the meantime had picked up her car keys and stormed off to the shop to exchange the chewing gum for a selection of chocolate bars and sweets.

★

The first day of term soon arrived. Clair was to report to Collingdean, a dormitory house, by four o'clock on a Sunday afternoon. She drove down to Kent with her mother, the school trunk safely packed in the boot of the car.

The school driveway was long and tree lined. As the car swept up to the front of the building and around the rosebushes placed in the centre to act as a roundabout of sorts, Clair got her first good look at the building. A large Victorian house, it stood on four floors – an imposing example of the architecture of its time. A stone staircase led up to the double front doors, which were wide open to reveal inner glass doors through which girls and parents were carrying school trunks and loose belongings up to the dormitories on the second and third floors.

Carol introduced herself to the housemistress who was holding a clipboard which contained the names of pupils who were being ticked off the list as they arrived. The housemistress crossed Clair's name through and told them that Clair would be in Collingdean dorm. She added that she would be up shortly to introduce herself properly and check off her belongings. Carol and Clair climbed a sweeping staircase with red carpet and gilt edges to the second floor and checked the names of the dorms written in black on each door.

They finally came across the dorm down a corridor and opposite a bathroom. This had a list of girls and days when they could have a bath pinned to its door. Underneath someone had scribbled, *Clean the bath out afterwards and rinse all pubes down the plughole*. Carol could barely walk for laughing and almost dropped her end of the trunk. Clair kicked open the door to her dormitory.

It was a large room containing four beds in all. Beside each was a wooden dressing table with three drawers. On the top of each dressing table was a red plastic tray. In one corner stood a sink with four glasses and built into the opposite wall was a small wardrobe. Each bed was covered with a blue and white striped canopy. Sitting on the bed opposite them was a girl who Clair guessed was a lot older than herself and must be a prefect of some sort. She had long dark hair arranged into two plaits and she introduced herself as Tracy. Clair found it hard to believe that she was the same age as this girl. She listened intently as Tracy told them that she had been at the school for four years, and that new girls were always put into a dorm with older girls who could look after them and show them around the school, introducing them to the new routine.

Carol thought this was a marvellous idea and hoped that the two would become friends. Clair found herself unfamiliarly tongue-tied in front of this new friend.

'You had better choose yourself a bed before anyone else gets here,' Tracy said, laying out a selection of school books and clothes on to hers to show everyone it was bagged. 'I'm off to see if anyone else has arrived.'

Tracy left the room leaving Clair and Carol to decide on a bed. There were three remaining: one on its own to the left of the room – 'Handy for the sink,' said Carol; one next to the door; and the third next to it but against a wall. Clair decided on the one by the door and directly opposite Tracy; she didn't like the one next to the wall and decided against the one by the sink because her mother liked it.

She bounced up and down on her chosen bed for a few minutes. The mattress wasn't too bad – not like her one at home, but Clair had a feeling that nothing here was going to be like at home. She grinned at the thought. This one's fine, Mum, just as good as home...

There was a sudden commotion on the landing outside. Someone else was coming and Carol and Clair both sat on the bed quickly to show that it was taken. A mother and daughter entered the room dragging a trunk.

'Here we are, Sarah,' said the mother. 'Collingdean dorm: Tracy Practice, Clair Hollands, Sita Patel and Sarah Premium.' She read the list on the door. 'That's you, darling,' she announced.

Spotting Carol, she held out a hand. 'Sandra Premium,' she announced, 'and this is my daughter, Sarah, it's her first day.'

'Carol Hollands,' said Carol, taking the woman's hand. 'And this is my daughter, Clair, it's her first day too.'

Mrs Premium turned to her daughter and said, 'Well, you had better choose a bed, Sarah, this one by the sink looks nice.'

'I'll have the one over there by the wall,' said Sarah for obvious reasons, and without a further word she sat herself down on it.

Carol and Clair looked at each other. Carol's mouth began to contort and Clair could see that she was finding this couple amusing. Not now, prayed Clair. Don't start laughing now, don't embarrass me now!

The housemistress they had met briefly downstairs entered the room and Carol pulled herself together.

'Good afternoon, girls,' boomed the woman. My name is Miss White. I am the housemistress here at Collingdean house, and I am here to help you, look after you and generally become your new mother during term-time.'

Suddenly Clair's and Sarah's mothers didn't seem too bad to the girls and Sarah Premium burst into tears. Her mother and Miss White rushed to put a comforting arm around the young girl's shoulders.

'She's a bit nervous,' said Mrs Premium, 'it's her first time away from home. Would you mind if I took her downstairs for a while? Perhaps a walk in the grounds would do her good.'

Miss White agreed, and Sarah, her shoulders shaking, was led away sobbing uncontrollably.

Miss White turned to Clair and said, 'Now then, don't worry about her; she'll be fine. Some girls get a little emotional at this point but they soon get used to the routine and we haven't had one runaway yet!' She laughed at her own joke and carried on.

'Right, young lady, as you can see you have a chest of drawers next to your bed. This is for your clothes, home and uniform – except for your Sunday suit and cloak, which must be hung up in the wardrobe over there.' She pointed to it and continued, 'On the top of the chest is a tray. This is for you to keep your belongings on so that the cleaners can pick it all up in one to dust. Now, if you could open your trunk we can start to tick everything off on my list and you can put everything away. The trunks then go down in the cellar until the end of term.'

Clair opened the trunk. Miss Green reeled off the list, putting a tick beside each required item.

'And finally,' said Miss Green, 'one hot-water bottle.'

'I haven't got one!' said Clair, desperately wishing she had.

'Oh,' said Miss Green, looking at Carol. 'We've got a tough one here!'

With this one sentence, Clair's fate was sealed. Without even trying, she had gained herself a reputation. She was 'a tough one'.

It was now five o'clock and Carol had to go. Kissing her daughter goodbye, she wished her luck and made her promise to phone the following evening. Clair said she would, and told her mother not to worry, that she would be fine and that she would see her in three weeks' time at the first exeat weekend.

Clair watched her mother drive away and waved until she saw her turn right at the end of the drive. Other girls' parents were leaving too, and she could see Sarah Premium in a car clinging to her mother. For God's sake, she thought, and went back upstairs to her dormitory.

It was empty, and trying to shake off a feeling of sudden loneliness, she sat down on her bed to wait, for what she didn't know.

Two girls passed down the corridor outside.

'I see we've got another fucking Hollands in the school,' said one.

'Not another one!' said the other.

Clair quietly digested this piece of information. Outside her family she'd never met another Hollands before. She wondered what she was like. Was she older? Was she younger than her, or the same age perhaps? She closed the door. She didn't want to hear any more. Not only was she a tough one but she was a fucking Hollands as well. This other girl must be a real pain. She hoped she wasn't in her class.

Opening her overnight bag she put baby lotion, cotton wool and a mascara on to the tray on her dressing table. She got out her collection of Enid Blyton books and arranged them proudly next to the tray. She had chosen a selection of albums to bring with her for use in the Common Room: Simon and Garfunkel's *Greatest Hits*, T-Rex, Queen's *A Night at the Opera* and her treasured David Cassidy album. There was a picture of him on the front sitting in a rocking chair and looking totally gorgeous. She kissed the front of the album and, unable to fit the records into one of the drawers, put them on the floor underneath the chest.

She put her toothbrush and paste into one of the glasses by the sink and went back to the bed again to sit and wait – for what, she still didn't know. She wished Tracy would come back, or even Sarah. She picked up the cuddly toy she'd packed for the bed: a large brown corduroy bloodhound called Oscar. It smelled of home. For a split second she wished she was there again fighting with her sisters.

Tracy and Sarah finally came back with another girl in tow. She was pale skinned and freckled with short ginger hair and was wearing flared jeans, basketball boots and an aertex sports shirt. Her eyes were the most startling shade of blue and her lashes were caked in more black mascara than Clair had ever seen in her life.

'You won't believe it,' said Tracy, her plaits swinging, 'you've got the same surname as Meggi! Meggi Hollands, meet Clair Hollands. Are you two related or something?'

So this was the dreaded other Hollands, was it? Well, she didn't look too bad to Clair. As it turned out she was all right. She was two weeks younger than Clair and in the same class. Her dormitory was opposite. It was for two people and she had been put in with a girl called Sarah Perkins – who, Meggi confided, she couldn't stand.

'I'm going to speak to Miss White and see if I can get moved,' Meggi informed everyone. 'She knows I hate Perky – she's got terrible smelly feet! Everyone knows that, and she's so square, she doesn't even like Rod Stewart!'

Meggi was a huge Rod Stewart fan. She had all his albums, and her only fault as far as Clair could see was that she didn't like anyone who didn't like his music. Clair told her she loved Rod Stewart almost as much as David Cassidy and she could tell by the other girls' faces that she was in, accepted as part of the group.

'Why do you call her Perky?' she asked.

Meggi answered, 'Sarah is the most common name in the school, so anyone called Sarah gets a nickname. There's Sarah Belgrave, she's Belly Balls, Sarah Snelgrave, she's sweet; we call her Snelly, and so on…'

Everyone looked at Sarah Premium. Sarah Premium looked at everyone. She had cheered up considerably and was beginning to like her new surroundings, but suddenly she wasn't too sure. She'd always liked her name and always hated nicknames. She waited. Clair took a good look at Sarah. Her brown hair was cut fairly short and particularly spiky on top.

'Who cut your hair?' asked Clair.

'Mum took me to Vidal Sassoon's, it's where she goes; why?'

'It's a bit spiky on top,' said Clair. 'It reminds me of a toilet brush!'

Everyone cracked up except Sarah.

'That's what we'll call you,' said Tracy. '*Bog Brush*!'

Sarah opened her mouth to complain, but the girls were saved by a bell – a loud one.

'Supper time,' said Meggi.

'Come on, we have to go down to the main school for meals.'

The girls left the building, but not down the main staircase the way Clair and Sarah had come.

'It's the back stairs for the likes of us,' Meggi informed them, and so down the backstairs it was. These stairs were quite different; there was no carpet on these, just pale blue slippery lino. The back door led out on to a stable courtyard and the old stables had been turned into the sixth-form block. It was every girl's dream to make it to the sixth-form. The routine there was far more flexible and privileges were great. Home clothes were allowed, and more hours for shopping in the village, and the best one of all – church on Sundays was no longer compulsory. The girls ran past the sixth-form wing with others joining them from every orifice of the school. Supper time, like all mealtimes, was a big thing in school life. The girls had to walk from the boarding house to the main school, which was situated a few hundred yards down the road. This building too had a long sweeping driveway. But the architecture was different. Constructed in red brick, it looked very eerie – especially at dusk as it was now. It also looked huge and alien to the new girls.

A cool September breeze rustled the leaves of the old oaks and the crows roosting in them barked out their calls to neighbouring birds with a gusto that unsettled the girls, who ran even faster to the safety of the school door, screaming and giggling with the excitement of their fear.

Clair had only been in this building once before, for her interview and entry examination. It had been held at the end of the summer term and Clair had been assigned a girl to look after her. The girl's name was Sophie Summer and Clair had thought she was the nicest person she'd ever met. Sophie was trendy big time. She wore her uniform skirt short, a sin in itself, and her blonde hair was cut into the latest 'shaggy dog' style. She carried the latest *Le sac* bag made from the top end of a pair of jeans, and a packet of cigarettes was stuffed into its back pocket.

Sophie knew the school inside out. She knew the rules and how to break them, and she had taken Clair under her wing with an enthusiasm, founding a friendship that was to last the girls a lifetime. Sophie had shown Clair around the whole school pointing out the relevant buildings and telling her all the best places to go for a fag. Clair didn't smoke but she realised that she had become privy to information which she somehow felt other girls attending their interviews might not have been trusted with. Clair liked Sophie and she was looking forward to seeing her again.

The girls ran into a back passage that led through to the dining hall. Other girls were everywhere, chatting and laughing catching up on each other's gossip, desperately eager to hear news of the summer holidays – who'd been where, who'd done what. The girls followed Meggi through to the dining room. There was a smell of mashed potatoes in the air.

Every school Clair had ever attended smelt of mashed potatoes. Two third-formers stood at the entrance to the dining room handing out free pots of Marmite. It was the smallest pot Marmite produced, a sample pot, and each girl was given one at the beginning of term. Clair thought it was really cute, a word she had picked up from her Canadian friend at home. Small though it was, she would have to make it last.

The dining hall was beginning to fill up. Tracy spotted an empty table at the far end and ran ahead to grab it. Clair looked around for Sophie; she couldn't see her anywhere and was disappointed. She decided to ask Meggi and Tracy if they knew her. They did. Everybody it seemed knew and liked Sophie. Meggi herself had had a pash on her for years. Clair didn't know what a 'pash' was, so it was explained to her that younger girls quite often had pashes on older ones who they admired. With some trepidation Clair realised that she must have one of these pashes on Sophie.

'But Sophie isn't older than us, is she?' said Clair, fiddling with her jar of Marmite on the table.

'Course she is!' said Meggi. 'She's in the fifth form, and she's been made a prefect this year and head of Collingdean. She's in Bodiam dorm with Snelly.'

Some third-formers came over to the table with trays loaded with four plates of supper for the group. It was shepherd's pie and a plate of bread and butter. A jug of water and plastic cups were already on the table.

The girls ploughed into their supper. Clair realised that she had been at the school for only a matter of hours, but she was aware that she was sitting with friends. These were people she felt she had known for years, and as she chatted happily and listened intently to her new friends, she realised that boarding school was living up to its expectations – and more. Once the shepherd's pie was eaten, the girls tucked into the bread and butter, spreading it greedily with the Marmite from their pots. Clair had just taken a big bite when two hands appeared from behind and covered her eyes.

'Clair, you got in then, poor old you!'

It was Sophie. Clair almost choked on her bread. Sophie was with two other girls and all of them were wearing jeans and huge baggy cricket jumpers; Clair and Meggi both made mental notes to get themselves one. The three sat down at the table.

Sophie introduced her friends to Sarah and Clair. They were Snelly and Brenda. Tracy introduced Sarah as Bog Brush, infuriating her immediately.

'It's Sarah, actually,' she said bravely.

'Oh, is it now?' said the three fifth-formers simultaneously.

Clair was feeling uncomfortable. Sophie seemed different somehow, not quite so friendly and most certainly older than her. They were letting their superiority be known, but Clair knew that becoming a fifth-former was an important stage in school life; it released you from the doldrums of being the underdog and catapulted you into the realms of bossy boots.

'Where did you get those pots of Marmite?' said Sophie.

'They were giving them out at the door,' said Tracy, who didn't have a pash on anyone and wasn't easily intimidated. 'If you'd been here on time you might have got one.'

'Well, we went for a fag and missed supper, I'm starving,' Sophie replied.

Stretching over to the next table to grab a plate from a delighted third-former, who definitely had a pash on her, she helped herself to three pieces of the bread and butter.

'Give us some of your Marmite,' said Sophie to Clair.

Clair didn't like the way she asked and, holding the pot tightly in her hand, she said no.

Sophie looked stunned. 'What did you say?' she asked.

'I said no.'

'Why?'

'Because,' said Clair, feeling herself going pink.

'Because what?'

'Just because.'

'Just because what?'

'Because, one, it's only a tiny pot and by the time you've put it on all that bread there will be nothing left and two, you didn't say please.'

'Didn't say please! Okay, please can I have some of your Marmite?'

'No!'

Sophie was getting pissed off. 'What are you, Jewish or something?' she said.

'No; actually, I'm not even christened,' Clair replied innocently.

Sophie, Brenda and Snelly almost wet themselves. Scraping back their chairs noisily, they got up and left the table. Sophie ruffled the top of Sarah's head in a friendly manner and said 'See you later, Bog Brush,' while giving Clair a superior look.

Bitch! thought Clair.

'You've got a lot to learn,' said Meggi. 'Come on, we'd better get back to Collingdean. Don't forget your Marmite,' she added sarcastically.

The first night at boarding school passed successfully enough. Meggi begged Miss White to be moved to a different dorm, but to no avail.

'No girls can be moved at this stage as you know very well, Meggi.'

'But Sita hasn't arrived in Collingdean dorm yet. Can't you put her in with Perky, and I can move in with Clair and Sarah?'

Miss White wouldn't budge from her decision and Meggi sulkily admitted defeat.

Monday morning, the first real day of school dawned bright and sunny for the girls. A bell sounded at seven in the morning and Miss White's assistant housemistress, Miss Good, popped her head around the door.

'Good morning, girls,' she said 'Time to get up! Quick chop – news notes by eight o'clock.'

As quickly as she had appeared she was gone, along to the next dorm with the same message.

'What's news notes?' asked Clair.

Tracy explained, 'We have to be over at the main school by eight to listen to the news, then we take notes and have to answer questions later. After that we go to the dining room for breakfast and then off to our classroom.'

Clair thought that news notes sounded like a good idea and gave Bog Brush a look that said so. Bog Brush wasn't looking, she was too busy laying out her uniform with pride on her bed.

Long grey skirt, long grey socks, blue shirt and grey itchy jumper, not to mention the big green baggy knickers that went over her ordinary ones and stopped the draught whistling up her legs. Bog Brush was proud of her uniform and she put it on with great dignity.

Clair laid hers on the bed too and decided that hers looked even better than Sarah's. She quickly dressed and they compared length of skirts – yep, they were still two inches from the floor as they knelt down together to compare. The final part of the operation was to put on the sensible black lace-up shoes. When each pair was safely on the girls' feet and tied in double bows, the girls were ready.

At that moment Meggi came bounding into the room. But what was this? Her grey skirt was short, her long grey socks were rolled down to form two grey tyres around her ankles and her shoes were most definitely not black lace-ups – they were platform clogs!

Sarah and Clair looked at each other and glared at Meggi. Clair instantly rolled down her socks, Sarah fiddled uncomfortably with the elastic of her big knickers and the four of them filed out of the dormitory and over to the main school in differing frames of mind. Clair's legs felt cold, but she couldn't roll her socks up now; that would really make her look like a wimp… but what would the teachers say when they saw her? Would she be in trouble? Help! Too late, they were in the main doors once more and making their way towards the dining hall for breakfast. The most revolting stink of boiled eggs hit the girls' noses as they walked into the dining room.

News notes came and went with the new girls, Clair and Sarah, scribbling for all they were worth and Meggi and Tracy chatting away in the corner of the hall with other friends catching up on the news. If a teacher looked as if she might be coming towards them too close for comfort the girls would quickly scribble something down, but by the end of the five minute news session, Tracy had written one line and Meggi had drawn smiley faces all over the first page of her new notebook.

Clair and Sarah had written their names neatly on to the front page of their books and had compiled three pages of news notes in their neatest handwriting. They were at a new school and they wanted to impress.

The first week was a mishmash of meeting other girls in their classes and the vast array of teachers who came and went with each passing lesson. Clair began to feel at home and to blend in with the other students, she relaxed her guard with regards to work and news notes. By the end of the first week she was limiting herself to one page of news notes and lots of smiley faces, much to the disgust of the teachers and the amusement of the other girls.

On the second evening Clair had phoned home to speak to her mother and had locked herself into the small cubby hole that served as a phone box at Collingdean house. The walls were whitewashed and clean and a small stool in the corner served as a seat for the girls as they chatted to parents, desperately shoving in further ten pence pieces for longer chats with home, their lifeline to the world they had left behind them.

Clair was describing the school and all its good and bad points to her mother when she noticed some very small writing in red ball-point pen at the top of the wall behind her.

'What does it say?' Carol asked.

'I can't read it,' said Clair, craning her neck.

'I'll climb up on the stool and see what it says,' she told her mother.

Leaving the phone to dangle by the box, she clambered up on to the stool and read the words that were calling to her.

'What are you looking up here for? The pips are going,' she read.

The girls had settled into a routine. Clair had learned to fit in with the others and to go along with what they thought and did within the school day. Sita had failed to return to school and so Meggi had got her way and been moved into the dorm with Clair, Tracy and Sarah. The four girls had become inseparable, like the Famous Five stories, only four. These books had done the rounds at Collingdean House and had been read by almost everyone living there from the fourth form down. The fifth-formers were too scary to offer the books to, although Clair and Meggi still secretly had a pash on Sophie and took every opportunity they could to suck up to her when the others, especially Tracy, weren't around. They would secretly offer to be her slave, and would run errands for the older girls, or take their washing down to the boiler room to dry or clean their shoes for them.

Occasionally the older girls would take advantage of the younger ones by making them agree to give them half of their tea. Tea was the best meal of the day at boarding school, and the most fun because it was held in the small comfortable surroundings of the boarding house kitchen rather than the more formal surroundings of the main school dining room. The younger girls were generally more than willing to share their tea in order to get in to the older girls' good books, especially Clair, who had learned to understand the advantages of having an older girl on your side. Except, that is, when the tea consisted of 'sticky willies' – boarding school slang for iced finger buns. These were served once a week and were like gold dust. Nobody ever wanted to give them up, and girls would almost certainly scoff these before their sandwiches for the sole purpose of keeping them, preferably in their stomachs.

Clair learned to smoke cigarettes, which were always called 'fags', and were obtained either by helpful day girls or by having the guts to put on make-up and home clothes and sneak out of school and up to the local newsagents, without being caught, to buy them.

Clair's only hiccup in school life had been during one break time when first learning to smoke.

She had been kneeling around a loo at the main school, sharing a cigarette with Tracy and Meggi, when she had decided to try tapping the accumulated ash with her right index finger, the way she had seen her mother do it. She had tapped too hard and managed to karate chop the girls' last precious fag in half in her enthusiasm.

The girls had said she was being flash. She was. The incident had got her sent to Coventry for the rest of the break and well into the succeeding science lesson. She didn't do it again.

One week seeped into another, until halfway through Clair's first term on one Saturday afternoon the four girls were sitting in the common room listening to David Cassidy LPs. They were bored. Really, really, bored. Saturday afternoon was the only time that they were allowed into the village to spend pocket money. They had to wear the Sunday suits of green cotton for these outings but were allowed to change into home clothes when they got back to school. All had put on their jeans and eaten the mountains of food they had returned to school with. They had listened to Meggi's new Rod Stewart album, had a pillow fight with the cushions which sat on the colourful plastic bucket chairs, paid for by school funds, and they were still bored. Then Tracy had an idea.

'Let's walk across the fields to Foxhill Farm,' she said.

Meggi groaned and said, 'What for, it's miles away and—'

Clair interrupted her. 'That's a brilliant idea! A couple of fifth-formers told me that the farmer's got a horse in one of his fields. We could see that and get some duck eggs and put them in with the eggs for breakfast, that would get a good laugh!' she said.

Meggi started to think it was a good idea. Sarah was up for it too, and the four of them started to plan their escape.

They decided to go out of the back of the building through the kitchen. No members of staff would be around that area at that time as they would be in the staff room except for Miss White, who would be on duty towards the front of the house and was organising a game of netball for the third-formers. Third-formers were another problem. There was nothing they liked more than to snitch on fourth-formers and get them into trouble with the housemistress. The girls would have to be on the look out for both these and staff members.

The next step was harder. The Head's cottage was within the grounds and the 'Old Hillbilly' as she was known was at home.

The gardens were structured in such a way that the only chance to get through them was down a path that narrowed into a green walk right past the Head's cottage.

'She's probably drunk and won't notice us,' whispered Meggi.

'I bloody well hope so,' Sarah whispered back wishing she had never agreed to come. Her mother would kill her if she got into trouble.

'For fuck's sake, stop whinging!' shouted Clair.

All four ducked behind a bush.

'Shut up, you idiot,' Tracy hissed to Clair. 'Do you want to get us all bloody caught, you stupid cow?'

'Who are you calling a stupid cow?' retorted Clair. 'You were the one who had the idea, it's all your fault if we get caught by the Hillbilly, not mine!'

The door to the cottage opened and the girls ducked.

The Hillbilly came out of the front door holding her cat. She looked around the garden and sniffed the air, hiccuping. Then she let the moggie leap from her arms and scratched her enormous belly.

The girls were too scared to move and didn't dare to speak. The hillbilly teetered over to a rose bush in her red high heeled ankle boots and checked the blooms. She called kitty back into the house and was gone, back through the front door from which she had come.

The girls stayed where they were, frozen with fear. Only after five minutes did they feel that it was safe enough to continue with their journey. They snuck past the windows at the back of the cottage one by one in army style. Then, still crouching, they ran as fast as their legs would carry them on and on through the orchard and on to the other side of it where they climbed a brick boundary wall and fell to the other side, only now feeling able to scream with laughter at their ordeal. Meggi and Sarah almost wet themselves; Clair did, which only made the other girls laugh even harder.

They lay on the grass, safe in the fields of corn, and planned the next stage of their journey. They figured they had about a mile to go across the fields until they reached the farm.

They kept running across the fields. This time the pressure was off and they could laugh and be themselves, revelling in their own mischievousness and laughing at their own childish jokes.

White clouds drifted across the autumn sky as they found themselves nearing the farm and the field that housed the horse.

He was a dapple grey and he was beautiful. The girls plucked large handfuls of grass to feed to him, but Clair wanted to get closer to him.

'I'm going in,' said Clair.

'Don't!' cried the others.

'He might not be safe,' ventured Sarah.

'Oh, shut up, Bog Brush, you wimp! If you don't try things, you will never know. *I'm* going over!'

She climbed the stile and boldly stood next to the horse.

'See, there's nothing to it, he's a sweetheart,' she called.

At that moment the horse reared and started to claw in the air with its front hooves above Clair's head. Tracy and Meggi started to scream. Clair began to run; the horse galloped after her and Clair dived into a huge hawthorn bush that was growing in the middle of the field. Here she stayed, terrified, with the horse whinnying and scraping at the ground with its hooves while trying to bite her through the prickles of the bush.

Clair started to scream for all she was worth. She screamed and screamed and screamed.

★

The girl in the red suit was still clutching the After Eight, which had long since melted in her fingers, and all four of her dinner guests were screaming with laughter. The waiter, having long since given up any hope of leaving early, had turned the music off and the lights up in the hope that his last customers of the evening would get the message and leave.

'We ended up having to call for the farmer, who came and rescued me. It caused a huge stink at the school. I was in tears, my legs were all scratched from the prickles in the bush, and I tell you what – I have never been near a horse again and never will, either!' Clair told them, scraping back her chair.

The others got up to leave. The waiter gave them their coats and they paid the bill.

Clair tucked her arm through her friend's and smiled.

'I like your suit,' she told her.

Cry War

The bombs had been exploding steadily around the hotel where the journalists were staying for the duration.

Although sounding off in the distant hills and lush valleys the explosions were clear and defined and frightening to even the most hardened war journalists.

For Paddy McCoy their sounds sent a sickening thud of anticipation to an already fragile stomach. It was Paddy's first assignment in a war-torn area and he had spent a year preparing for it and participating in the training necessary, which was organised by the British news bureau he worked for. Paddy had wanted this job desperately. He'd been deemed fit for it by a chief editor he worked with and had known since his University days.

He was an experienced journalist, having made his way up through the ranks of local papers and on to three nationals before realising his ambition to join a well respected and professionally dedicated bureau for its war dispatches department. It was said that any part of the world only had to cry war in order for journalists to be let loose on the next available flights to airports abroad, closed or otherwise.

There was always a way in for journalists, and for Paddy, on this his first occasion, the airports had thankfully been open and not too damaged, with a large UN presence around them. The other thing that had guaranteed Paddy the job was his deep understanding of the warring parties' culture and the fact that he spoke their language fluently.

But now, sitting on the loo with a damnable stomach bug brought on by the country's lack of proper sanitation, he was beginning to wonder if it was all worth it. He and his colleagues from the agency, along with journalists from the BBC, ITN and leading British and foreign newspapers, had been stuck at the hotel unable to venture out to where the new stories were happening for the past six days. Tempers and nerves were wearing thin owing to the frustration of only being able to dispatch small amounts of copy through the limited number of satellite contacts set up in hotel bedrooms and makeshift newsrooms.

People were everywhere inside the hotel, going about their business – some reciting, some typing copy, but all being kept busy in an already deteriorating country; they were all missing their families and wishing they could go home.

Some journalists were being recalled because of the increasing danger of the situation surrounding them. Paddy (thankfully, he thought) was not being asked to return to England, but was getting ready to send some important copy when his stomach had called him to the loo on more pressing business. Leaving the loo, he ran into one of his colleagues, Andrew Smith. Andrew, unlike Paddy, had a wife and three small daughters waiting for him back home and was not savouring the moments away as much as Paddy.

'Where have you been?' asked Andrew. 'They've just bombed an ammunitions dump up in the hills and London is screaming for a story!'

'Stomach flu,' said Paddy, his guts still wrenching. 'But don't worry about it, we'll get the story for London even if it kills me.'

The once smart tiled reception area of the hotel was by now a hive of activity. Satellite links were being set up and journalists from different parts of the world were buzzing about between the reception area and the downstairs bar area, which had been turned into a makeshift newsroom ready to send out copy as it was radioed through to them by other newshounds on the scene shortly after the blast.

Looking around him at the live broadcasters waiting to send messages to television stations around the globe, Paddy was glad he was working in print. It meant he could sit down write his copy and send it down the line without having to make sure he looked the part or even in some cases change his shirt and put on a tie for the occasion. Paddy was a good writer. Precise and fast, he soon had the story for London and managed to get it sent through quickly and directly.

When evening fell on the hotel, sounds of gunfire could still be heard into the distance although much more faintly now. Hostilities seemed to grind to a halt during the night, a fact which all the people in a war stricken land could be slightly grateful for. However, all were ever fearful for their lives in a civil war that made no sense to the everyday people who lived there and, some said, was beginning to make little sense to the men who had signed up to fight the battles raging through towns and villages alike.

Paddy was sitting in the bar enjoying a Scotch when something happened that would change his future. A sudden surge of rapid gunfire was heard coming from the front of the building followed by a deathly silence. The front doors of the hotel situated in the reception area suddenly flew open and two women each clutching a child, burst into the hotel.

Paddy was the first to reach them. They were panting and breathless a look of fear was in their eyes as they both fell to the floor in front of him. One of the women, who seemed to be in her forties, started sobbing uncontrollably. The small boy she was holding clung to her like a young animal in fear of its life. The other woman, younger than the first with dark hair and mascara-stained eyes, was the first to speak.

'Please help us, the soldiers want to kill us and we must get away, we need help, please help us,' she begged.

Andrew had followed close behind and tried to reassure them.

'It's okay, you're safe now,' he said to the two women.

Lifting the younger one gently by her arm, Andrew assured the woman that the danger was over.

Paddy lifted the older woman to her feet and two female journos who had joined the group carried the children downstairs to a corner of the bar area and set them gently on a sofa. Their mothers followed trembling and scared and sat down with the children whispering soothing messages into their ears, each one stroking her child's terrified face.

The affect of the drama on the newsroom was startling. The journalists were used to travelling to where the stories were happening. To have a story come to them was new, different and exciting, and they all scrambled around the party on the sofa, all of their trained noses smelling for the story unwinding in front of them.

Paddy decided to take control of the situation.

'Come on, you guys,' he said to the twenty or so people who had gathered around him. 'For Christ's sake leave them alone. Can't you see these people are terrified?'

'There's a story here, Paddy,' ventured one member of an outside broadcasting unit, his cameraman already filming beside him.

'And what makes you think this is exclusive to you?' he continued.

Paddy looked at the two women's scared faces.

'It's not exclusive to me, but these people need to rest – anyone can see that. They need to talk to someone in authority about what's happened to them,' he said.

The newsman wouldn't be put off. Waving at his cameraman to stop filming, he argued, 'Oh, and you think you're the one for the job, do you Paddy? I think this is a case for the United Nations or the Red Cross. These people could put all our lives in danger if whoever was taking pot-shots at them decides to come back.'

'Well, screw you mate,' said Paddy, who was now on his feet, fuming at the profession he had chosen and its representatives. 'These people have come to us for help and I'm bloody well not going to send them back outside to God knows what!'

The two women were beginning to cry again. The older one was sobbing uncontrollably into her son's hair. The scene around them became silent. Andrew took the initiative and cleared the area.

When everyone had dispersed Andrew and Paddy began gently to question the two women. The older woman was called Maria and her four-year-old son's name was Carlos. Neither spoke a word of English but the younger woman, Stella, did and quietly explained that her three-year-old son Christopher and her friend and child had been gathered up from their village and made to walk for two days and nights with little rest and hardly anything to eat.

Trembling, Stella told the journalists that all the men in the village had either signed up with the army or had been rounded up by enemy forces and taken to unknown destinations.

The women's husbands were part of this round-up which had taken place over two months ago. Neither woman had seen or heard from their husbands since.

After being rounded up themselves, they had agreed to try to escape as soon as possible and had run down the hill towards the hotel when they saw its lights in the distance. The soldiers had not realised they were missing at first, but tipped off by other members of the group hoping for a favour, they had given chase firing at them indiscriminately in the dark.

'All we want to do now is escape to Dula. It's a town about one hundred miles south of here,' Stella was explaining. 'It has been designated a United Nations Safe Area. I have friends there, we'll be safe.'

'What about the soldiers in the hills?' ventured Paddy, 'Won't they come looking for you?'

'They won't dare,' explained Stella. 'They know there are foreign journalists staying here and won't want to cause any trouble here; besides, they will be long gone now, walking to God knows where with our neighbours.'

Just as she had said, the soldiers did not return that night and relative silence filled the midnight air.

Paddy decided that the women and their children should be given a hot meal and put to bed in one of the hotel's many unoccupied bedrooms.

With the newcomers settled in their beds and the remainder of the hotels guests dispersed, Paddy and Andrew sat up in their room deciding what to do.

The room was twin-bedded with a chest of drawers between the beds and a wardrobe in one corner. A door led off to a bathroom, and a small desk in front of the heavily curtained window played host to a word processor, paper and a selection of pens, notepads and tape recorders.

Paddy was sitting at this desk tapping a pen on its wood. Andrew was lying on one of the beds with his hands crossed behind his head. He had given a lot of thought to the problem and had decided there was only one thing to do.

'We've got to help them,' he said, sliding across the bed to grab a cigarette from the bedside table.

'I was thinking exactly the same thing,' replied Paddy. 'But there's no point in us both going; besides, one of us is going to have to stay here to continue sending copy back to London. They'll smell a rat if we both disappear.'

Andrew drew long and hard on his cigarette, blowing the smoke out slowly before he answered.

'It's going to have to be you, mate. You speak the language, which is going to be a definite plus in this situation.'

The two men decided that the party should make an early start and so retired for the night with the day's events still buzzing in their heads.

When Paddy tapped on the women's door at six the following morning it was quickly opened by a fully dressed and still frightened Stella. Paddy slid inside. The room was neat; the beds had been made and the other woman and the two children were sitting on a bed staring at the man before them.

'I'll take you to Dula, but it will be a dangerous journey,' he said. 'Do you think you can cope with it?'

Stella's eyes brightened. 'It will be worth it,' she said.

The small party gathered outside the hotel while Andrew went to the underground car park to fetch the vehicle that was to be used for the journey. A few cameramen were on hand to record the event, while wishing Paddy and the women good luck for the journey. The children were placed in the back of the Jeep – two innocents in a pointless war, lying on blankets and pillows placed in the back for their comfort.

'The tank's full of petrol,' said Andrew, 'and there are two cans in the back. God knows if you'll be able to get any more, but with luck this should get you there.'

Paddy loaded maps, water and food into the front of the vehicle and Stella got into the front passenger seat next to him. The other woman sat in the back between the two young boys.

Goodbyes were said, and the car slipped away on to the forest road and made its way slowly along the winding lanes that led to the main highway. Once they were on the highway they found the roads had cleared of snow and the journey was made easier for the party.

The roads were empty and for a whole hour of their journey the five saw no other vehicles. None of them spoke, preferring instead to be left to individual thoughts, dreams and fears.

Paddy finally broke the silence.

'I can't believe how clear the roads are, Stella. Any idea what's going on?' he asked.

'There are no towns or villages in this area. This is, or was, part of our most beautiful countryside. We must keep our eyes peeled, though. We can never tell who's watching us from up in the hills,' Stella replied.

Paddy shivered to himself. Looking up at the hills all he could see were snow topped mountains and lush forest. She was right, it was a beautiful part of the country. Paddy consulted his map. They had made good time. If they continued at this pace they could reach Dula in five hours.

The children, who had been sitting quietly in the back, were getting restless. They both needed the loo, so Paddy pulled over to the side of the road and they all got out. The children walked on to the grass verge to relieve themselves. Paddy stretched and lit a cigarette. He offered one to Stella, who accepted it gratefully. Suddenly Maria, who had walked further up the verge, came back towards them trembling and retching. Paddy ran up the bank.

Lying face up with a look of terror on its face was the body of a woman, the victim of a landmine. Wasting no time, Paddy retreated and bundled the others back into the car. Maria held the children close to her and quietly sobbed. Stella was looking at Paddy for an explanation.

'Dead body,' he said. 'Let's get out of here.'

He pulled two bars of chocolate out of his rucksack and passed them to the children before slamming the car into gear and retreating from a small part of hell in beautiful countryside.

Silence once again enveloped the car, the travellers retreating to their private thoughts. The afternoon sky had been blessed with a good amount of sunshine, brightening the landscape. Other vehicles had started to join them on the road, and the map showed that a small town was coming up, which possibly explained the increased volume of traffic. United Nations vehicles, their white paint dirtied by splashes of slush, started to appear in the distance. A UN roadblock had been set up and Paddy eased the car to a halt near the soldiers on the side of the road.

'Where are you heading?' asked one of the soldiers, his steel grey eyes peering at them from under his beret. He was Irish.

'I'm Paddy McCoy, British journalist. I'm taking these people to Dula. They've escaped from their captors and have friends who can help them there,' he explained.

The soldier didn't flinch. 'Papers!' he commanded.

'I've got mine,' said Paddy. Theirs were taken away from them when they were captured.'

The soldier walked away to discuss the matter with his commanding officer. After some pondering and looking in Paddy's direction, the officer came over to Paddy.

'We shouldn't really be letting these people through without the proper papers but we've heard about their plight and so we have decided to turn a blind eye this time,' he said.

Paddy was astonished. 'How on earth have you heard about us?' he asked.

'The story has been flashed across the world. Some of your people got hold of it. You're quite a hero, sir.'

'Andrew...' sighed Paddy. 'Ah well,' he said, laughing, 'you can't blame him for doing his job.'

'Keep driving for about another hour, sir, and you'll reach Dula; the roads are clear. There's no reported trouble at the moment – things are pretty quiet,' said the officer.

Stella's face lit up at the news and she turned to her friend whispering gently the words that the soldier had said. For the first time in forty-eight hours her friend allowed herself a smile and started to sing gently to the two children.

A weight was lifted from the party's shoulders. The journey had gone remarkably smoothly. Paddy in particular had imagined that it would be a lot more dangerous than it had been. The roads were once again clear and he put his foot down on the accelerator, eager to get to Dula, eager to get these people to safety and the comfort of their friends.

The road forked to the left and a battered and war-weary sign told them that the town was a mile away. Soon the lights from the town's streets and buildings could be clearly seen. One more UN roadblock to pass through and they had arrived. As they drove into the town the change of pace was instantly remarkable. People walked happily along the streets. A smell of food being cooked hung heavy and tantalising in the air.

Paddy parked in a side street and helped the women and children out of the car. The first priority was food and the group decided to find a restaurant in order to sit down in the warm before moving on to the homes of the two women's friends. The restaurant was bright and lively and warm. A log fire crackled against one wall and students sat around it drinking and laughing. There seemed to be so much cheer and very little to worry about. These were definitely people who felt cherished and safe, clothed in the blanket of the United Nations.

Paddy ordered soup and bread all round and watched as the colour returned slowly to the children's cheeks. The two women had addresses for their friends and were excited at the prospect of seeing them again and having somewhere safe to stay.

All were in a state of disbelief at having made their escape and all without exception were eternally grateful to Paddy. But as the friends sat chatting and eating and the students by the fire had started to sing traditional songs, high in the hills above Dula a rebel army was planning to tear apart their already fragile lives.

The makeshift camp for the fifty-strong force had been erected and camouflaged throughout that afternoon. An armoury had been established and each man carried a rifle and held a box of ammunition. Tempers were running high and the commanding officer, a slightly built man with small black beady eyes and a shock of grey hair, was pacing up and down shouting orders to his men with the ferocity of someone obsessed. And obsessed he was – obsessed with making a name for himself in this bitter and bloody turmoil he called a war.

The commanding officer knew that Dula was a proposed Safe Area; but that had been an agreement made between the UN and an army that he had since deserted. He was trying, in his madness, to alienate the army from his group of men in order to try and achieve his own goals quicker.

We are only fifty now, he thought to himself, but soon others will hear of our glory and we will become bigger and stronger: a more powerful force.

A 130 mm shell had been loaded into a field gun and was primed and ready to fire on to the town. The officer took a swig of alcohol from his flask and ordered the gun to be fired.

Within a minute of his order the shell was hurtling through the clear night sky towards its unsuspecting destination.

Paddy had paid the bill and was helping Maria and Stella back into their coats. Most of the people in the restaurant had started to sing, and from what seemed like nowhere musical instruments had appeared and were being played with the enthusiasm and gusto practised before the war.

As Paddy took one glance back on the scene, he was almost loath to leave this place that seemed so full of hope for the future. They picked their way through the tables that stood on the streets outside the café and made their way up the road towards the car. Stella turned to thank Paddy once again for all he had done.

Paddy looked into Stella's dark eyes. He had become very fond of this brave woman over the past two days and found himself wondering if she would be happy with the friends she planned to visit.

'There's no need to thank me any more,' he said. 'I was glad to help, and besides it seems as if this might make a good human interest story back home. Hopefully, it will go some way towards making our Government rethink their part in this war.'

Stella's eyes welled with tears. Impulsively, she put her arms around Paddy, and they held each other in a mutual understanding sometimes shared by men and women. At that moment the shell landed on the pavement in front of the café. The blast blew away the front of the building. Bodies and body parts were everywhere, and the screaming that ensued sent shock waves through the town. Maria and the children fell to the floor with the force of the blast and lay there too stunned to move.

Stella fell into Paddy's arms, her eyes wide, and she looked into Paddy's face once more. A slight smile momentarily lit up her face before her eyes closed and her body went limp in his arms. A large piece of shrapnel lay embedded in her back.

High in the hills above Dula, a commanding officer congratulated himself.

Window Pains

David Tyler parked outside the house and checked the address in his diary: 112, Compton Villas. This was it all right, he'd got the right address. He checked his notes: windows and a back door. Wiping the condensation from his windscreen he looked at the building. The windows were falling out of the large Victorian terrace house and the paint was peeling. As the wind blew on to the gables he could see the frames shaking from the shock. Perfect – it was ten o'clock on a Monday morning and it looked as though the week might be getting off to a good start. These people definitely needed double glazing. Packing his diary and tape-measure into his briefcase, David got out of his car and locked the doors behind him. He took the path to the front door and rang the bell. The door was opened by a woman in her late sixties. Her hair was dyed a light purple and neatly permed. She was wearing a flowery summer dress over which clung an apron. Under her arm was wedged a small dog that yapped savagely at her visitor.

'Mrs Benson?' David enquired.

'Yes, dear.'

'David Tyler, Costalot Windows.'

Blank expression.

'I have an appointment with you this morning, new windows and a back door.'

'Yes, of course,' said the old woman, throwing the by now hysterical dog into the understairs cupboard and beckoning David through to the kitchen.

'I've been expecting you,' she added.

David followed Mrs Benson into the kitchen. Pale blue painted Sixties wall units greeted him. All the Victorian features had long ago been eradicated, and the room in the old woman's mind some thirty years ago had no doubt been nicely 'modernised'. David noticed that the far wall of the kitchen was taken up with a large pine dresser and wondered if the old dear realised its value. This too had been painted the obligatory blue and was hung with blue and white striped cups and plates. Sixties originals no doubt – presently making a big comeback in Habitat, David had noticed on a recent trip into town.

The red formica-topped table which took centre stage in the kitchen, was laid out for breakfast and the old woman was removing bacon and fried eggs from a frying pan on the stove and laying them out carefully on to two of the striped plates.

David couldn't believe his luck. He hadn't eaten that morning, having overslept, rather having not been woken by the baby, who had overslept. 'Dreadful when the baby doesn't go off,' his wife had joked.

'I'll just give Brian his breakfast,' said Mrs Benson, 'and then I'll be right with you.'

Bang goes the breakfast, thought David. 'Who's Brian?' he asked.

Mrs Benson took the frying pan over to the sink and ran the cold tap on to it causing a turmoil of spitting fat and smoke.

Brian's one of my lodgers, dear,' she said.

She walked to the kitchen door and carefully closed it.

'Meet Brian,' said the old woman. 'Brian, meet – er, what did you say your name was, dear?'

David stood and stared at Mrs Benson and back again at the door. Pinned to it was a giant poster of Brian Tilsley from *Coronation Street*. Alarm bells started to go off in the salesman's head. Uh-uh, a nutter! Play it cool, humour her. No harm done yet.

'Er, Tyler, David Tyler. Pleased to meet you, Brian.'

Mrs Benson looked suitably delighted that the pair had met, and sat down at one of the chairs by the table to eat her breakfast. She beckoned to David to sit and poured him a cup of tea. She then poured one for herself and Brian, carefully plopping six lumps of sugar into the poster's stewed liquid, three for herself and – 'Not for me, thanks,' said David.

His instinct was to run, beat a hasty retreat – go back to the office and murder the telephone canvasser who had made this appointment for him; but the first rule of double glazing kept him under starter's orders: 'Every customer is a potential sale and every sale is a commission.'

It could be that the old woman was loaded and had retained enough of her marbles to understand that she needed windows. Could be that there was a sale here.

'Um, Mrs Benson, I really ought to be getting on with measuring your windows now,' he said.

'Plenty of time for that later; you haven't said a word to Brian yet. He's a bit quiet lately. He's left his wife Gail and is staying with me for a while until he can sort things out at home,' she explained.

Wiping fried egg from around her mouth with her apron, the old woman continued, 'Actually he's quite famous, you know. Actor.'

She said the last bit slowly and with pride.

David persevered.

'I have another appointment in half an hour and I really must get on with the measuring. If you could just show me where you want me to start. Upstairs perhaps? With the bedrooms…'

Receiving no answer, David continued with a standard sales patter.

'All our windows and doors are double-glazed and made from the finest plastics. We give a ten year manufacturer's guarantee and if you place an order with us within the next two days we are running a special offer at the moment that entitles you to free gutters and soffits on the outside of your property.'

Mrs Benson smiled sweetly at her visitor, and said, 'That's nice, dear. Yes, you go ahead on upstairs and do your measuring.'

David got a brochure out of his briefcase.

'Perhaps you and, er, Brian would like to have a look through this while I'm taking the measurements. It shows you the different styles of windows we can make for you – and here at the back are the doors we can supply. I'll just away upstairs then,' he said.

Mrs Benson took the brochure and started to thumb through it.

'Very nice!' she said. 'Go on up, but be careful not to disturb my other lodgers…'

'Jesus Christ, not more!' muttered David, as he took his tape-measure out of his case and tentatively made his way up the stairway.

A long bleak corridor landing greeted him at the top of the stairs with doors leading off on either side. All the doors were open, allowing liberal shafts of sunlight to penetrate the dark hall. A slight smell of violets hung in the air. From downstairs David could hear Mrs Benson deep in conversation with Brian, but apart from that there was a deathly eerie silence to the top landings that he was now creeping down.

He turned right into a large front bedroom, afraid and yet curious as to what he might find. The room contained twin beds with matching candlewick bedspreads. Nothing unusual there. In between the beds was a dressing table. On the dressing table were two alarm clocks and two glasses containing dentures. From somewhere in the corner a wardrobe door suddenly creaked open and David was out of there. With the ability of a sprinter he took the stairs two at a time and ran to the kitchen.

Grabbing the brochure from a startled Mrs Benson, who had forged it into a rather splendid looking hat, he grabbed his case, made his excuses and left. The dog, still locked in the cupboard, woke up as the front door slammed and did its pieces. David was out. He made his way back to the office with a murderous look in his eyes.

David arrived at work halfway through the weekly sales meeting. Storming across the showroom floor, not wishing to lose his anger, he ignored the receptionist and barged into one of the back offices where he knew the meeting would be taking place. As he opened the door thick cigarette smoke hit him. Behind a desk sat Pete, the owner of the company. On chairs arranged in a semicircle around him sat the sales team – five of them in all, all smoking and all talking at the same time.

'Who the hell made my appointment for Compton Villas, a Mrs Benson? David shouted. 'The woman's a nutter, loony tunes material! There's no chance of getting an order out of someone like that. It's been a complete waste of time. You are going to have to get those bloody canvassers to vet who they call a bit better! This one's got a Brian Tilsley fixation.'

David sat himself down on an empty chair.

'Brian Tilsley?' said Pete, drawing on his fag and adding his bit to the room's pollution. 'Do you mean Brian Tilsley from *Coronation Street*?'

'Well I can't think of any other bloody Brian Tilsley, can you?' David snapped. 'She's got a poster of him in her kitchen and she thinks he's real! She made him a cooked breakfast and made me sit down and have a chat with him.'

'A *chat* with him,' said Pete, intrigued now. 'How did he look to you?'

David gawped at him. 'He looked tanned and gormless, he looked like a bloody poster, what do you think?' he replied.

'Oh, I only wondered,' said Pete, winking at the others, 'because Brian Tilsley isn't in *Coronation Street* any more, they stabbed him dead years ago. So, given the circumstances I thought he might be looking a bit rough...'

Everyone in the room dissolved, and even David had to see the funny side.

'Has height,' came a muffled voice from the back of the room, 'Hyan Hilsley was hilled of ears haho, hest hing hey hever hid.'

It was Eddy, the only non-smoker in the team. Eddy objected to the offices having no windows or suitable ventilation and had taken to wearing a builder's dust mask over his face during meetings as a form of protest.

'Take that stupid mask off,' said David, 'and we might be able to understand you!'

The meeting broke up. The salesmen were given last week's sales figures and told in no uncertain terms what was expected of them sales-wise for this week. Pete promised to talk to the appointments co-ordinator about Mrs Benson and slowly the team trickled out of the office and towards the back of the building which housed the kitchen and the all-important coffee pot. David and Eddie poured themselves one and Eddie took off his mask. The kitchen had a window and he opened it, taking in huge gulps of fresh air.

'He ought to do something about that office,' said Eddie, referring to Pete. 'Bloody window company, and he can't even organise a window in his own office!'

'He's probably having too much fun winding you up about it, mate,' said David with a laugh, helping himself to a chocolate biscuit.

Keith, a veteran salesman, sloped into the kitchen looking grey and depressed as usual and poured himself a coffee in silence. He'd had a bad weekend. His fourteen-year-old stepdaughter had beaten up a friend of hers at the weekend and the police had come round to his house to give her a stern talking-to. To make matters worse he'd received a letter from the other girl's parents that morning which contained a letter his daughter had written to theirs, describing in graphic detail how she had lost her virginity.

The covering letter said that his daughter not only had a screw missing but a hymen as well. Keith had misread it at first and thought it said hymn. He'd then looked the word up in a dictionary and become even more depressed. An almighty row with his wife had ensued, and he'd escaped as he so often did to the security of the office.

He'd already told Tina, the receptionist, to give him as many evening appointments as possible and anything that came in for Saturday. He wanted out of the house, and he was going to make sure he stayed out.

Eddie stared at Keith's depressed shape sitting slumped in a chair pulling at the knot in his tie, and nudged David. David and Eddie didn't like Keith. He was a smarmy bastard and they'd had a lot of fun over the years winding him up. They'd recently discovered that he was screwing the receptionist and hated him even more for that, partly because they were cross at being the last to find out and partly because she'd never given them so much as a glance in their direction.

'What's up, mate?' David asked, putting an arm around his colleague's shoulders. Keith explained about his bad weekend and the letter.

'Jesus, that's terrible!' said David. 'Listen, I might be able to help you out with this one.' David turned and nodded to Eddie and again in the direction of the sink. 'I got given some really good coke this weekend, really pure stuff. It's yours, mate – help see you through this black spot.'

Eddie liked this one. They'd done it before. Quietly, he reached down to the cupboard under the sink and got out a container of Vim. Discreetly, he shook some of it into a piece of kitchen towel and added a small amount of sugar. David slid one arm behind his back and took the packet from him.

'Here we go, mate,' he said, 'one hundred per cent pure, this. Take the edge off things for you.'

Eddie closed the kitchen door and Keith shook the powder on to the table. David got a ruler out of the desk drawer and started to chop at it, earnestly sliding the powder into two lines. Keith found a straw left over from a trip to McDonald's and snorted the imposture up both his nostrils.

'Jesus, that's good stuff!' said Keith, rising suddenly and straightening his tie. 'Wow, I can feel that working! You're a good mate, David. See you later, chaps, I'm off to get an order.'

'Don't come back without one!' chorused Eddie and David, quoting the company slogan.

Keith strode towards the front door stopping at reception for a moment for a quick whisper with Tina and then was gone.

'Gullible bastard!' said David.

The back door swung open and two burly fitters entered the room. Henry and Sid were the best fitters the company had and worked like Trojans in rain sleet or snow to get their jobs done on time. Customers loved them and they would often boast to the other fitting teams of the lovely jam sponge Mrs so-and-so had baked for them for their elevenses today, or of presents they'd been given, or tips they'd been offered and taken. Today they were finished early and were seeking out David.

'David!' said Henry. 'Just the bloke. Mr and Mrs Black, Belvedere Close. That one of your jobs isn't it?'

'That's right,' said David, 'Pat and Les, whole house and a porch. Had to organise finance for them, though. Why, what's up?'

'Fucking pigsty, that place! Never seen such an 'orrible dump. Mess everywhere. We've been there since eight this morning and not so much as a cup of tea. Diabolical fucking dump that one. Missus was still in her dressing-gown when we left.'

David interrupted. 'I just sell the windows, Henry, I moved some dirty washing off the sofa, sat down and did my bit. What happens after that has nothing to do with me. If you've got any complaints, see Pete!'

'No no, no complaints,' chipped in Sid. 'Henry just wants to tell you what happened when we fitted the back bedroom window... go on Henry, tell the lads what happened when we fitted that back window.'

'Well,' said Henry, 'I'm on the inside and Sid's on the outside up the ladder, ain't that right, Sid?'

'It is, Henry.'

'Anyway,' continued Henry, 'We've got the window in, lovely snug fit it was, and I'm screwing it in place from my side – ain't that right, Sid?'

'It is, Henry.'

'I get to the last screw and I'm holding it in my mouth like I do when I goes and drops it and it falls down the back of some little Herbert's bed.'

'Tell 'em what happened next, Henry.'

'What happens next is I pulls the kid's bed out to retrieve the screw, don't I – I wouldn't have bothered, but it was the last one we had on the van, ain't that right, Sid?'

'That's right, mate.'

'So I pulls out the bed and there's the screw, slap bang in the middle of a pair of underpants, slap bang on the top of the biggest skid mark you've ever seen in your life! Well, I ask you what would you have done?'

David and Eddie exploded. Their laughter attracted the attention of Pete and Tina, and they came into the kitchen to see what all the fuss was about. David and Eddie left the fitters to tell the story again and picked up their appointment sheets from the front desk.

Eddie was scheduled for a Mrs Divine in fifteen minutes. She lived on the other side of town and he would have to move it to get there on time. He climbed into his Volvo.

Mrs Divine. What sort of a name was that? he wondered. Taking a short cut he knew he sped along the road and past the park he used to visit with the kids. God, that seemed like a long time ago. What was he thinking, it was a long time ago! They were both at college now and doing very well. Times had changed. He'd changed, too. He was older and greyer and still selling double glazing for a living. Not for the first time he thought about the possibilities of getting out of the business. But what would he do, what *could* he do? He had no formal training in anything. He was a salesman. It was what he was good at. He'd stick with it for now and think about it again later.

Eddie pulled up outside the house and checked that he had his tape-measure.

The house was a neat Edwardian semi in a very upmarket part of town. The windows were original sash and, Eddie noted, in very good condition. He hoped he wasn't wasting his time with this one. The house seemed to be in very good order; the front garden was neat and in bloom and a blue Mercedes sparkled in the driveway. No chance of dirty underpants under the bed here… Eddie chuckled to himself as he remembered the fitters' story. He rang the bell. *Greensleeves* immediately rang out from a box above the door. Tacky, always very tacky, these doorbells. But, a good sign. Doorbells that played tunes in his experience, more often than not spelled money – and that usually meant a sale. He straightened his tie, ran a hand through his hair and waited. He was listening to a second rendition of *Greensleeves* when the door was finally opened by Mrs Divine.

'Darling, I'm so sorry I took so long to answer the door, but I've been tied up all morning. You are the man from the double glazing company, aren't you?' she gushed.

Eddie held out his hand. 'Edward Sargeant, Costalot Windows – and don't worry about it, Mrs Divine, I've been fully entertained by your wonderful doorbell. '*Greensleeves*, wasn't it?' he said amiably.

'Quite possibly, darling, quite possibly! Do come in. I was so delighted when your lovely girl phoned me and suggested that I have new windows. It's something I've been thinking about for absolutely forever but never seem to get around to organising.'

She paused to open the door to her sitting room and beckoned Eddie inside. Pure, unadulterated opulence greeted him. Deep pink wall-to-wall Wilton carpet covered the floor. Two sofas in a gold stripe sat majestically on either side of a cast-iron Victorian fireplace inset with tiles. A marble topped coffee table stood in the middle and on top of this sat an onyx ashtray and matching cigarette lighter. The windows were decorated with pink festoon blinds; these always reminded Eddie of huge frilly knickers. Something classical was playing on a system in the corner. Eddie tapped his suit pocket to make sure he'd got his calculator. This was looking better and better.

Mrs Divine sat on one of the sofas and crossed one shapely leg over the other. Eddie sat down opposite her and started to remove the brochures and order forms from his briefcase and lay them neatly on the coffee table in front of him. He then got out a pen, retrieved his calculator from his pocket and laid these out neatly too. Eddie liked order. Like most double-glazing salesman he was superstitious. Some liked to wear their 'lucky ties' or arrange their desks in the direction according to *feng shui,* but Eddie liked to have the tools of his trade laid out neatly and in a presentation order. Mrs Divine gave a slight cough from her side of the table.

'Is this going to take long, darling? Only I've got poor old Mr Johnston tied to the bedpost, and he gets a bit fidgety if I leave him for too long,' she remarked.

Eddie wasn't sure that he'd heard her right.

'Poor Mr who?' he enquired. 'Tied to the what?'

'Mr Johnston! Terribly sweet, he is, just likes to tie me to the bed for half an hour while he reads me something by Harold Robbins. Apparently his wife can't stand what she calls those filthy mucky books in the house; though between you and me, darling, I've read worse. Then I tie him up for half an hour and pop back every ten minutes to shout at him. He's been coming to me for three years and the routine never changes. Anyway I'll be back in a minute...'

Mrs Divine left the room leaving Eddie to take it all in. She's a madam, he deduced. Unbelievable! She's got me here at the same time as one of her clients and she hasn't so much as batted an eyelid over it. The surrounding opulence of the sitting room suddenly turned decadent to Eddie. He heard a door in another part of the house opening and Mrs Divine's voice shrilled out.

'You naughty, naughty old carpet-bagger! How *dare* you bring those disgusting filthy books into this house? It's no good crying, I'll be back in ten minutes and if you haven't got rid of them by then, you're in *big trouble*!'

She glided back into the room and resumed her place opposite Eddie.

'There we are,' she said. 'That's that done! Now we'd better get on with windows.'

'Um, did you have an idea as to which ones you wanted changed, Mrs Divine? It's just that you've got original sash here, and we can make sash windows in the same style as these, with the major difference of course being that they are double-glazed. You'll notice a big difference with regards to noise and loss of heat and of course they are completely maintenance free.'

He paused.

'Well,' said Mrs Divine, 'I would eventually like the whole house done, of course, but I think I'll start with down here for the time being. Perhaps this room, the dining room and the kitchen. Best not to go into the room next to the kitchen and disturb Mr Johnston, but I've had that room soundproofed anyway, and it's always lovely and warm in there – no problem at all with heat loss.'

Eddie picked up his tape-measure and notepad and said, 'I'll start in here, then.'

'Wonderful, darling. And make sure you give me a good price! I'd hate to have to put my prices up to afford them, and if at the end of the day I can't afford your quote, poor old Mr Johnston might get a bigger ticking off than he bargained for! Now you carry on, and I'll get you a cup of tea.'

'That would be lovely,' said Eddie.

He took his tape-measure and started to work out the measurements for the bay window. He jotted them down and measured the side window. Leaving the sitting room, he ventured out into the hall. The kitchen was at the end of it and Mrs Divine was busy there making the tea. He turned left into the dining room. More frilly knickers hung in the window, and he quickly measured it and made his way towards the kitchen.

'All done in the sitting room and dining room,' he said. 'I'll just measure up in here then I'll sit down and work out some prices for you.'

'Oh, that was quick,' said Mrs Divine, putting chocolate fingers on to a plate on the tea tray. 'I'll take these into the other room for you and be back when you've worked it out.'

Eddie measured the windows, being careful not to knock any of the ornaments off of the sill. He jotted down the measurements and headed back down the hall in search of his tea.

Mrs Divine was nowhere in sight but the tea and biscuits were on the table as promised. Eddie gulped down the tea and ignored the biscuits. He picked up his pricing book and started to work out the prices on his calculator. Picking up an order form he drew small diagrams of each window and wrote its price neatly in the box beside each one. Having worked out the overall costs, including VAT, he got his portfolio out and waited for Mrs Divine to return. She was back almost immediately and Eddie wondered if she'd got the room set up to a video camera somewhere.

She sat down and picked up her tea.

'So, darling, what's the damage? Am I going to have to put my prices up?'

'Er, no! No, I don't think so,' said Eddie, and laughed. 'I think you'll find that we're very reasonable. Here's the price, as you can see, for the bay and side window in here, and dining room and kitchen windows. The price comes out at five thousand two hundred pounds, inclusive of VAT.'

'Well, that's not as bad as I thought it was going to be,' declared Mrs Divine. 'Yes, I'd like to go ahead with that. I presume you'll require a deposit?'

'Well, thank you very much,' said Eddie. 'If you could make out a cheque for thirty per cent of the cost, I'll go back to the office and arrange everything for you. We should be able to fit within six to eight weeks, but our surveyor will come along first to take accurate measurements. That should be sometime next week.' Eddie handed her his portfolio. 'If you'd like to take a look in here we've taken some rather nice before and after shots of other people's properties, and it will give you a good idea of what to expect.'

Mrs Divine took the portfolio and started to look through it. Just then the door opened and a tall chap with dark hair greying at the temples popped his head round the door.

'I'll be off now then, Kitty,' he said. 'See you next week.' And with that he was gone.

Mrs Divine handed the portfolio back to Eddie and looked at her watch.

'They all look beautiful,' she said. 'But I really must be getting ready for my one o'clock appointment; he likes me in the nurse's uniform when he arrives. I look forward to receiving a written quotation from you, though, and thank you so much for coming.'

Eddie packed everything back into his briefcase and, clutching his cheque for the deposit, he made his way to the front door. Mrs Divine let him out and he got back into his car. The one o'clock appointment arrived and rang the bell.

This time, *Home, Home on the Range* rang out from above.

Home, Home on the deranged, thought Eddie, shutting the car door.

I really must get out of this business.

Have You Seen the News, Mummy?

The television was still repeating the warning when Kate had thrown the last tin of food into the tartan shopping trolley. It had continued to repeat it as she ran into the garden and threw herself momentarily into her husband's arms.

Steve grabbed the children. The little one, objecting to being so rudely disturbed from his game in the sand, cried for the hell of it. His sister told him to shut up. She knew what this was all about. She had been told that a war to end all wars, was imminent. Granddad had said so.

With a wisdom way past her eight years she ran alongside her father as though her life depended on it. It did.

Kate reached the bunker at the end of the garden first. As she ran, from somewhere in the distance she heard a scream – a blood-curdling access of emotion that she knew had involved great courage. She unlocked the heavy grey door. Throwing the shopping basket in ahead of her, she switched on the generator. Once, twice she pumped its button until the room glowed golden to reveal their unwanted home.

'Twenty-five foot by fifteen, Mrs Brown.'

That's what the man from Nuclear Bunkers PLC had said as he trampled through the mud to the designated area.

'That's government rules and regulations, not the company's. Twenty-five feet and a chemical toilet. That's EU regulations, of course; Swiss made, they are – very nice. Choice of colour, white or blue,' he continued.

He'd sworn as his trouser leg caught on a bramble.

'They'll have to come up, for a start! This whole area will have to be cleared and dug down to six feet. It's for the concrete you see.'

He had said the last bit kindly, seeing the hurt that was now creeping across Kate's sunburned face.

The work had taken eight weeks. It went on all through that summer and into September. By December, bunkers were going up faster than Christmas trees and negotiations with 'Sod 'Im' as the enemy was now called were no nearer to any kind of an agreement.

Watching the news had become a way of life for everyone. For the children it was an irritating inconvenience which disturbed the pattern of normality.

'Have you seen the news, Mummy?' Flora would whine, clutching a bedtime story. But her mother could only cry.

The room was indeed twenty-five feet by fifteen. Two sets of bunk beds lined the far end of it. Blankets and pillows sat quietly on top in anticipation. A pine refectory table covered in a cloth decorated with strawberries stood by the door, above which sat a larder filled with tins. A sofa and an armchair to the middle of the room, with a rug on the floor, suddenly – in the face of death – looked ridiculous.

They had brought them home on top of the car.

'We'll want to be comfortable,' Steve had joked as they drove the mile home. They had both collapsed in fits of laughter at the sight of themselves struggling down the garden, one each end of the sofa, the dog yapping at their heels.

It had all seemed so funny then. The threat was over. The Prime Minister had assured them of it. But suddenly, as quickly as it had gone, it reappeared like a cancer in everybody's lives.

Now, standing at the door staring at the sofa, Kate suddenly felt sick. A wave of nausea hit her temple just as Steve and the children reached the room, Flora collapsing on to the sofa with her face red and sweaty from the run.

They all sat in silence, each to his or her thoughts. Kate's mind turned to Mrs Levy next door. She had lived there for thirty years.

'But it's all over, Kate, you have nothing to worry about now,' her neighbour had assured her with a hint of a Polish accent.

'It's not,' said Kate, angry now at Mrs Levy, angry at the Prime Minister, the world. 'It's not over, it's very real, and we want you to come into the bunker with us when the time comes!'

Mrs Levy had slowly picked up her knitting. After a while she said, 'A kitchen table saved me during the last war, dear.'

Leaving the knitting, she led Kate into the kitchen. The glass panes of the Victorian sash windows had been painted white. The kitchen table in all its glory was supporting three panelled doors. Underneath, laid out neatly on the tiled floor, was a pillow and a pink quilt. Lined up in tidy rows by the side of the pillow were tins and an opener.

'The man from the council gave me a leaflet, dear,' she had explained.

Kate had left Mrs Levy's house an hour before the warning. Now, holding Josh in her arms, she visualised her neighbour sitting under the table on the pink duvet, knitting. A lone, unasked for tear made its way slowly down Kate's face.

Outside cars lined the streets – some empty, others filled with frightened people; some screaming, others silent. A dog made its way along the pavement. Somewhere in the distance a baby cried.

Inside the bunker the family sat. A flash of whiteness lit the afternoon sky followed by absolute silence.

Sea Views

The ice cold water hit the girl's face like a slap from the past. She had been asleep. Now, suddenly faced with danger, she was wide awake, coughing and spluttering. A slow realisation of what had happened, of what was crossing her face and dripping from her drenched hair, came to her. The gold satin sheets she was lying in were slowly turning a chocolate brown from the liquid that was seeping into them.

Looking up, she saw her pimp marching into the *en suite* bathroom. The large hand-painted bowl she used to keep her make-up in was in his hands as he crashed it down on to the tiled dressing table built into the mahogany sided bath. Louise noted that the make-up was all over the floor as she pulled herself quietly up on to her haunches.

'You little bitch!' said the pimp, now standing over her with his hand raised. He wanted to hit her but knew that he couldn't. He could never risk marking the pretty face that was now looking up at him with a blank and dull expression, or colour the eyes that were now staring at him with a look of pure hatred.

'Go on then, bleedin' hit me, why doncha?' she said, pulling the top of her pyjamas over her head. 'No, you wouldn't do that would yer, you bastard! You wouldn't do anythin' that other people might notice. Nothin' that would let them suss out the real you!'

Grabbing a clean T-shirt from her wardrobe, she left the bedroom and headed towards the spiral staircase that led from the landing of her mews house to the sitting room. Reaching the bottom and taking a familiar glance at the sea views, she plonked herself on to a leather sofa and picked up the handset for the TV. She punched the numbers on the remote control and the set jumped into action. Breakfast television was into its first half-hour, and Anthea Turner was telling her viewers that all women know how it felt to have a bad hair day. Louise, her hair still dripping, only half smiled at the irony. She looked up from the television to see Frank coming down the stairs holding a peach coloured head towel.

'Dry your hair off,' he ordered, throwing the towel at her.

As Louise wrapped her long red hair into the turban she was creating on her head, she began to wonder where it had all gone wrong. It had all started that summer. She had met Harry on the beach. A smile unwittingly crossed her face as she remembered the first time they had met. There had been no wind that summer, which was unusual for the seaside town she lived in. Sea breezes, the locals called it. Howlin' bleedin' gales was Louise's preferred description.

It had been five o'clock and most of the locals and all of the holidaymakers had left, or were packing up their picnic baskets and deckchairs and heading for home or hotel. At the same time the fishermen were starting to gather on the beach, setting up their rods in anticipation of the mackerel that swam close to the shore at that time of the evening, and were easy pickings for professional fishermen and children alike.

Louise had taken off her shoes and was walking slowly through the surf, cooling her feet, her distinctive hair cascading down her back. She was thinking of nothing at all when a golden Labrador had come bounding through the surf to meet her.

'Hello, friendly,' she said bending to stroke his wet back. 'What are you doing here then? Cooling off like me, I shouldn't wonder.'

Holding the hound by his collar Louise looked up and down the beach for an owner. Squinting from the sun she saw a figure running down the beach holding a lead. As he came closer, Louise noticed that his face was round and tanned and, she thought, not at all unpleasant to the eye.

'Is this yours?' she called.

'For my sins,' said the stranger, peering at her from under his baseball cap. Louise held out her hand and told him her name.

'Harry,' he responded, adding a quick, 'how do.'

It had all been so innocent. That summer they had shared a relationship that had grown into a passion which neither one of them had asked for or anticipated, and yet both wanted and needed to restore their sanity and block out the real lives waiting for them away from the solidarity and mystery of the small town's beaches.

That first meeting, Louise reflected, had been somehow a turning point in her destiny. A time of innocence, and wonder at how a past that had been peppered with prostitution and violation could, indeed did, give way to show a young girl there was love to be found in the world and stable relationships to be had, if she looked in the right direction.

Harry had looked at Louise with interest. He had never seen anyone quite like her with her red hair, pale complexion and piercing blue eyes not unlike his own.

He had asked her if she would like to go for a cup of tea at the small café in the park adjacent to the beach. She in turn had accepted with very little concern for herself or her well-being. After all, what harm was there in having a cup of tea with a good-looking stranger in a public place? Her only fear was Frank. Were he to find out that she was socialising with what in his mind could be defined as a potential punter, his temper and the darker side of his nature would surely come back to haunt the girl he had taken care of for the past ten years of her life.

Frank Skinner was a spiv in the Second World War sense of the word. His clothes were always neatly ironed; his shirts were from Bond Street and his jackets always smart. He came from a poor background where he had been the youngest of eight children of Roman Catholic origin. As a child, he was constantly dressed in his elder brother's cast-offs, and only experienced his first pair of new shoes at the age of eleven for his first Holy Communion. This fired his thirst to always wear the best clothes money could buy and to always earn the most money his obsession for garments to cover his back would allow. This money, he had decided, could only come from pimping. He was thirty years old and had seen a vast number of girls come and go through his high-class prostitution service; but never in ten years had he seen or had anyone as special as Louise. He loved her, he hated her and he commanded her in a way that was as abhorrent to him, with his Catholic background, as condoning abortion would be to a priest.

He was mixed-up, screwed up and confused. He had never allowed himself to become involved with his girls and yet here he was, after a relationship that spanned a decade, finding himself head over heels in love not just with one of his slags, but with Louise.

She in return had betrayed his trust. She had also betrayed what he saw as a stable relationship, the nearest he imagined she would ever come to a proper family environment. He was her family. He cared for her, clothed her and fed her. He lined her up with the most suitable punters and offered pastoral support when her clients got nasty. If they got too unpleasant, he ordered in the heavies to sort them out, to make them realise that they could not treat Frank Skinner's girls in that way and get away with it.

He was mother, father and friend to that girl and she had betrayed him. She had got involved with another man on a personal and – to Frank – improper level. He saw her as being obsessed with this man, and it broke his heart and tore at his soul more than any other thing had done in his whole life.

Louise was a fifteen-year-old misfit when Frank had picked her up close to London's Victoria Station.

It had been easy. She was wearing faded blue jeans and an American footballer-style top proclaiming the number 74, and she was leaning against a bus stop chewing gum. Even at such a young age she was obviously streetwise and clued in to life on the edge in London. But best of all, she was beautiful. Frank Skinner stood at a bus stop opposite hers and kept watch over his prey for ten minutes. He admired the way she could turn heads and simply ignore the drunks who staggered down the road towards her.

He had walked over to her and asked her if she'd ever considered a career in modelling, at the same time giving her his business card. This told her his name and named The Star modelling agency at an address in Soho where he could be contacted. After an initial meeting with him at his then run-down offices, Louise realised that modelling to Frank Skinner had different connotations. She was quick enough and streetwise enough to realise that 'Stars' was a front for escorting, and she had quickly become one of his highest paid and most popular prostitutes, commanding fees that ran into the hundreds. Her contact book boasted judges, MPs and policemen alike.

Her popularity was such that Skinner had moved her to the seaside town and put her up in a smart and well-furnished house to accommodate his important clients. This could afford them a retreat away from the stresses and strains of their careers into the peace and serenity of a country house with sea views. All this he had supplied for Louise, along with the most beautiful clothes money could buy, and now after a decade of moulding and sculpting his Muse, he was faced with the prospect of losing the one thing that he had ever truly loved: his woman, his little girl, his love, his property.

⋆

The waitress served the tea with an air of disinterest only compatible with someone very young who was filling in time before going to university. Leaving a tray of tea, cups and hot water she tore a page from her receipt pad and placed it on the table where it stayed until the tea was drunk.

Louise said she'd be mother, and steadily poured two cups for herself and Harry.

'Nice spot, this,' he said, looking out of the large windows that surrounded the café. 'Nice and peaceful.'

'Yes, I suppose it is,' said Louise. 'You kinda get used to places, really. Don't appreciate them as much as visitors.'

'How did you know I was a visitor to the town?' asked Harry, holding his cup like a mug.

Louise laughed. 'Oh, when you've lived here for a couple of years like I 'ave, you tend to notice the tell-tale signs,' she said.

'Go on, then, tell me what mine are,' said Harry, amused by this beautiful girl with her cockney accent and stunning good looks.

'Well, you've got yer bleedin' dog with you for a start, and you're kinda dressed as though you prepared for a walk along the beach. There doesn't seem to be anything spontaneous about you,' she explained.

Harry was grinning at her now. She was right, damn it! It both annoyed and amused him that someone he had only met half an hour before could have formed such a precise judgement about him.

Harry was thirty-six years old and had just ended a four-year relationship with a shallow, selfish woman who always seemed to be talking about her hair, or her make-up, or the latest fashions and the benefits of Levi's jeans.

Harry had become so bored and so outraged by her shallow outlook on life that he had just up and left her in the middle of a Sunday afternoon. He'd loaded his dog and a suitcase into his car and left. He'd driven down the motorway until he reached the seaside town and booked himself into a hotel paying cash for a week's booking with an option to stay on if necessary.

It had taken some persuading for the hotelier to take the dog in, but after discussions they had agreed that it could stay in an outhouse in the grounds of the hotel at night, to be reunited with its master every morning.

Harry had left his lady and was preparing for a new stage in his life. He didn't know what exactly was in store for him but he knew two things: he didn't miss her and he didn't care. He phoned his partners at the graphic design studios he ran in south London and told them he would be away for at least a week. His partners were confused by his sudden departure but quite capable of running the business without him, and so humoured what they saw as a thirty-something's need to relive his youth. Besides, Rachel had already been on the phone to them that morning shouting the odds and accusing them of a conspiracy to split her and Harry up.

This only served to amuse one of Harry's partners, who had never liked Rachel, and decided to have a little fun with her – reminding her that she could now spend all day in the bathroom doing her hair, and telling her that his wife wanted to recommend a new shampoo she'd found, in order to finally get her off the phone.

With the tea drunk, Harry picked up the bill and paid at the cash desk near to the entrance of the busy café. There he found children demanding ice lollies and parents wiping sweaty heads and tugging at sweet-stained infant hands, leaving the café for their weary journeys home.

Harry and Louise were by now totally comfortable in each other's company. The bill paid, they climbed the stone steps that led from the park to the beaches above. They walked a few hundred yards to where Harry had parked his car and agreed to meet again the next day.

As Louise walked the mile home, she was euphoric. She realised that Harry was special to her and that she had done the one thing that she had never imagined would happen to a girl from her background: she had fallen in love. This realisation signalled the beginning of a change within the girl who, in her youth, had been shown no love from a drunken mother, and had never experienced a relationship with her father who had left home before her birth.

Her euphoria was only marred by a fear that Harry might find out about her past, her occupation and – worst of all – Frank Skinner. As she made her way through the almost deserted streets of the town to her home on the south side, Louise decided that the time to act against her chosen but unwanted world was now.

She walked up the steps that led to her Georgian town-house and put her key into the lock of the large black door. Her mind was buzzing. She knew that she had to tackle Skinner. She knew that she owed him for a living that had kept her in a style she had become accustomed to, but realised with a sudden surge of relief that he did not own her. Louise knew he could not ban her from living the life that she eventually chose, and that if she did not choose to continue with prostitution, there was nothing, she decided, he could do to stop her.

It would be hard, she knew; it would be a fight, but she realised with some anticipation that the only thing stopping her from a life of love and self-fulfilment was Frank.

Entering the black and white tiled hallway, she threw her keys on to the maple occasional table in the corner and took the spiral staircase up to her sitting room.

The cleaners had been in and the rooms smelled of furniture polish and Briwax. Fresh flowers had been placed in the various vases that decorated the sitting room and the french doors that led to a small first-floor balcony had been left open, allowing a soft breeze to enter and the curtains to move slightly in the summer breeze.

Kicking off her shoes, Louise reached for the telephone. The first thing to do was to arrange for some time off in order to give herself the opportunity to spend more time with Harry. She dialled Frank's number in London, and his secretary answered the call.

'Hello, Skinner Enterprises.'

'Rosie, it's Louise. Is Frank there? I need to talk to him urgently.'

'Oh, hi, Louise! Yes, he's in, but I'll warn you now, he's in a foul mood,' said Rosie. 'Some of his bouncers at one of the clubs got themselves into a bit of bother last night, got a bit heavy-handed with a couple of blokes trying to get in without ties. Frank's been on the blower all day to his brief trying to sort it all out.'

Louise sighed. That was all she needed, Frank in a filthy mood with aggro on his plate.

That would mean that she would be lumbered with him for the weekend, drowning his sorrows in a bottle of her whisky. She was going to have to handle this very carefully.

'Hello, baby,' said Frank.

Hearing his voice made her jump momentarily.

'Hi, Frank! I hear you've had some grief over the night-clubs this week,' she said, trying to keep her voice neutral, afraid of letting the mask slip.

'Nothing I can't handle, sweetheart, and certainly nothing for you to worry your pretty head over,' came the reply.

'Does this mean that you'll be coming down here this weekend?'

'No, I think I'm going to be pretty tied up here for the weekend, I've got this and a few other problems to sort out.'

Eureka! Louise could hardly contain her joy at hearing these words. Now all she had to do was to break the bad news to him.

'Frank. I need a couple of weeks off from the business. I'm tired and I need some time to myself to think things over.'

There was a long pause on the other end of the line before Frank answered.

'What's brought this on, Lou? You know I've got you lined up with some very important clients next week, arrangements have been made up here that can't be easily broken,' he began.

Louise had started to shake, but her voice when she replied was clear and precise.

'I need a break, Frank. I've been doin' too much. There's too much goin' on in my life and I need to spend a couple a weeks sorting my head out; I don't know if this is the business for me any more.'

Frank exploded. 'Not the business for you any more! What the fuck are you talking about? It was the business for you ten fucking years ago, was it not, when your mother had chucked you out and I found you on the streets practically potless, so what the fuck has got into you now?'

Louise kept her voice calm. 'Get Rosie to cancel all me engagements for the next couple a weeks, Frank. I told yer I need a break.'

Slowly, Louise put down the receiver. She was shaking. God knows if he'd bought it. She poured herself a large Scotch and turned on the TV.

Frank Skinner slammed down the phone and stormed out into the reception area to Rosie, shouting, 'Cancel all Louise's appointments for the next two weeks. Soppy cow reckons she needs a holiday!'

Rosie jumped to attention, immediately picking up the phone to do her job, a job she did well, and had decided she could do well without this week.

Frank stormed back into his office slamming the door behind him. Inside, he poured himself a large whisky. Sitting at his desk, he leaned back in the large leather boardroom-type chair and downed his drink in one. What has come over her, he wondered? In all these years she had barely taken any time off, preferring instead to work hard, keep her nose clean and to the ground.

'Sod it,' he said out loud. 'One more problem with bloody women is all I need.'

He flicked on the intercom on his desk and spoke. 'Rosie, line Suzi up with all Louise's clients this week; she's been begging me for a better clientele.'

Clicking off the intercom, Frank Skinner rose from his seat and walked to the window. Staring down at the busy streets below, he made a mental note to himself to call down and surprise Louise towards the end of next week.

Saturday dawned bright and sunny for Louise. Drawing the curtains in her bedroom, she looked out of the window to see a few elderly people and holidaymakers walking eagerly along the pavements to their various destinations.

Dressing quickly, she brushed her hair and tied it loosely at the back. She had agreed to meet Harry on the beach at eleven. It was ten thirty and that gave her plenty of time to walk down to the rendezvous point opposite the steps of the café.

As she walked she wondered if he'd be bringing that daft dog with him again. She rather hoped he would. She'd never been allowed pets as a child, and now that she had her own home she had decided against one, because she spent so many hours away from the house and thought it cruel to keep pets unless she was able to give them all the attention they needed.

She walked along the promenade and past the Martello tower which had been put up to protect the beaches during the Second World War and was still standing, now used as a museum. She noticed that there were three ice cream vans along the first stretch of beach today. Expecting a weekend rush, she deduced. Harry was sitting on the wall that ran along the promenade waiting for her.

The dog lay panting from the heat at his feet. Harry was delighted to see Louise. He had been able to think of nothing but her since the night before and his heart and loins ached for her to be near to him. He knew that she was the woman for him, and for the first time in his life he wanted the whole caboodle: love, marriage, and – dare he even think of something so *passé* – the horse and carriage as well. He was a man sworn to bachelorship since his university days. But the thoughts that were going through his head now surprised and even shocked him, as he watched Louise's slender frame walking gracefully towards him.

'I'm so glad you're here,' he said, holding out his hand to hers.

A smile fit for a king lit up Louise's face. A warm glow enveloped her and she knew that she had fallen in love, totally and unequivocally in love, with someone she had only known for twenty-four hours. She had read, indeed been told that it could happen, but had never dared to hope that would happen to her. Harry took her hand in his and rose to his feet.

'I've missed you,' he said.

I've missed you, too,' she replied. 'I was afraid that you wouldn't be here.'

The next week flew past for the couple, with Harry's outlook on the relationship being the same as hers. He loved everything about her: her sense of humour, and the way she was able to get on well with all the people she met. He loved the small town that was as unaware of her profession as he was; the townspeople knew very little about the girl with the long red hair, except that she lived in one of the largest and oldest properties in the town and, some of her neighbours guessed wrongly, was married to a tall well-dressed chap who worked abroad a lot – a reference to Skinner.

Their small-minded deductions went unnoticed by Louise, who largely kept herself to herself. She tried not to spend too much time socialising with the townsfolk, except to pass an idle time of day with some of the shopkeepers, always terminating such chats when they came dangerously close to the topic of her life, or Frank, or the smart cars that were sometimes parked outside her house.

Harry and Louise had now become a couple. They spent the week laughing, talking and exploring the town and its surrounding country villages. They visited pub gardens for long and luxurious lunches, and cosy intimate restaurants for soulful and secretive dinners.

Louise finally took him back to her house, and after days of professing their love for each other, they finally made love together during one sunny afternoon. It was during this afternoon that Frank Skinner decided to climb into his Jaguar car and surprise his protégé.

As he was driving down the motorway, Louise was under the covers with Harry. After years of treating lovemaking as nothing more than a job, she was finding out the true meaning of the word. She was discovering that men were not all bad, but could be loving, thoughtful and gentle.

Harry was in heaven. He adored every part of Louise's slender body, and exploring it for the first time left him with a feeling of sheer joy. He caressed it, adored it and wanted very much to own it, in a way he had never done or wanted to own anything before.

As the couple lay quietly in each other's arms, with her satin sheets draped over them, Frank's car glided to a standstill outside the house.

Frank walked up the steps to the front door and let himself in with his key. He took the stairway to the first floor sitting room and threw his briefcase on to one of the sofas.

Seeing no sign of life, he walked quietly up the next flight to the bedroom and walked in.

Louise was the first to see him. Too shocked to speak, she could only stare at Harry, her love – the one thing she wanted more than anything. He in turn looked from Frank to Louise and back to Frank.

Before Harry could utter a word, Frank Skinner pulled out a revolver and shot him dead.

His body twitched once and then lay still, a pool of blood spilling from his wound on to the sheets.

Louise lay in stunned silence, not daring to move, too shocked to speak.

Quietly, Frank went to the phone next to her and dialled a number.

'It's Frank. I'm at Louise's. I need a body taken care of.' Quietly he replaced the receiver, and lifted Louise from the bed.

Within two hours the body was gone, the bed and sheets changed and Louise was back in them being given a shot to sedate her by one of Frank Skinner's doctors.

The ice-cold water hit the girl's face like a slap from the past.

The Competition

The doctor's waiting room was crowded as usual. Laura had decided to make an appointment for the twins even though she knew it was probably just a virus. A virus – how many times had she heard that one she wondered? It was the doctor's favourite description for anything that involved a headache, fever or runny nose. The twins had been off play school for three days and had done nothing but loll about on the sofa watching endless videos of *Playbus* and *Rosie and Jim*. Eventually Laura had phoned the doctor's surgery.

'I can fit them in on the emergency list, if it's a genuine emergency,' the receptionist had informed her.

Laura didn't think that a virus constituted a genuine emergency, if there was a genuine emergency she would call an ambulance, but she told the receptionist it was and was told to come in before eleven. The surgery ran a numbers system and Laura was given the number twenty-eight. She looked at the plastic card. Twenty-eight! Good grief, she could be there all day.

'How many doctors are on duty?' she asked.

'One,' replied the receptionist.

'How many people are there in front of me?' Laura continued.

'Twenty-seven,' replied the receptionist.

Laura sat down for the long wait, the twins scrambled out of their double buggy and as usual made a remarkable recovery. Why do children always manage to make liars out of their parents? Laura wondered, as she watched her sons roly-poly up and down the waiting room floor. She got up and gave the receptionist back her number.

'I think we'll leave it,' she said.

She took the long way home through the park. Perhaps this was all the boys had needed – some fresh air and an outdoor play. They were probably as sick of being stuck in as Laura was. She sat herself down on a park bench. The twins ran to the slide and climbed up. They never showed the least bit of fear about anything. They loved climbing, and they climbed everything – furniture, trees, anything which would invariably give their mother kittens in the process. But she loved them desperately, and could hardly remember a time when she didn't have them to keep her company. They were four years old, and very appealing. Everyone on the estate loved them and they were made a big fuss of wherever they went.

Laura had lost her husband when she was eight months pregnant – he'd had an accident on the building site where he'd been working. There had been some compensation, an out of court settlement. It wasn't much. But enough to buy everything she had needed for the babies and to put some by to live off. Not much for a life though, she knew that. She had been twenty-one when the accident happened and had been married a year. She was twenty-five now and quite often felt older and frumpy. She needed cheering up; a make-over would be nice.

She had often seen people work wonders with worse cases than hers on the television. They took all sorts of people from all walks of life and quite literally transformed them, though she often wondered how they looked when they woke up the next morning. Was the hair still gorgeous, or sticking up in all the wrong places? Did they spend hours in front of the mirror, feebly trying to duplicate the make-up after spending a fortune on the products used for their transformations? Or did they eventually relent and go back to their scrubbed pink faces, using soap and water when the sample face creams and toners ran out, and – most defeatist of all – did they let their hair flop back to the middle parting it had formed all their lives? That all amounts of coaxing and tressing were powerless to stop in its determination for the ordinary! The ordinary, that's what Laura's life was. Ordinary in the extreme, and hitherto subconsciously, but lately more and more in the forefront of her mind, she wanted it changed.

The boys were starting to wilt under the excitement of a trip out and a run in the park. Laura strapped them back into the buggy and made her way home. She could see the rooftops of her estate from the park, across the rolling green fields and huge oaks which made up the sublimity of a quiet playground between the two South London towns so hungrily surrounding it.

Laura followed the path that ran through the middle of the park and came out by the railway line. The fast train to Victoria hurtled past with speed, and startled the boys out of their limbo between sleep and the need for lunch, signalled to them by the time clocks in their brains.

'Train!' screamed Jack, 'Train, train!'

George, not wishing to be left out, joined in. 'Train, Mummy! Look train!'

Laura pushed on past the station and out on to the main road. The traffic was heavy and fumes hung thick in the air; a bus passed by slowly, chucking out a steady stream of exhaust. Laura pressed the button at the pelican crossing and waited for the traffic to stop. She crossed to the other side and carried on past the flats and was grateful that neither of the boys wanted to get out and walk the low green painted railings that surrounded their perimeters.

They loved walking on these railings, or rolling down the grassy banks beyond, although Laura had stopped them from doing this recently after Jack had rolled through some dog shit on the way to a friend's birthday party. The mess had been smeared all down his jeans and no amount of wiping away or scrubbing with a J-cloth had managed to get rid of the smell completely, leaving the mother of the house with a pong to get rid of long after the children had gone home.

Laura smiled as she remembered that at this same spot last winter, George had sneakily thrown his balaclava, which he hated and said made his head itchy, away on to the pavement, only to have a little old lady come racing along on her walking sticks to deliver it back to a grateful Laura and a totally bemused George.

The local shopping precinct was crowded and the usual array of teenagers let out of school for lunch sat chattering on the concrete spiral staircase that climbed up the middle: 'An architectural masterpiece of the Sixties,' someone had once told her; but now a convenient place for kids to gather on or hide behind to sniff glue.

Laura kept going. Her house was only two minutes' walk away now and she couldn't wait to get back. The boys had thankfully fallen asleep and that would buy her some time to make them some lunch before they woke up again.

The house was as she had left it, a mess. The washing-up had not been done. Toys were strewn all over the kitchen floor and out into the hall, making a kind of Hansel and Gretel trail into the lounge, ending at the empty toy chest.

Laura picked everything up and threw it all back into the chest, furiously. The toys were the only thing about having children that Laura could never quite get used to. The bloody things got everywhere: bricks, balls, soft toys – all over the house, all the time. And the worst culprit of all the dreaded Lego. Lego was banned. One small box of it had come into the house at Christmas and was in the bin by Boxing Day.

'In order to save my sanity,' Laura had told her sister when she had expressed disappointment at the decision.

But the toys did have their useful moments, like now, when they could be used to take out the anger of a wasted trip to the doctor's. The last one was thrown into the box and Laura went to tackle the kitchen.

With a necessary speed she'd washed up, wiped down the sides, swept the floor and was just starting to make the sandwiches when the boys woke up and let themselves out of the confines of the buggy.

Laura folded it up and put it in the cupboard under the stairs.

'Lunch will be ready in two minutes, you two, so don't go getting all those toys out again,' she called.

'We won't, Mum,' said the two together. They quite often said the same things at the same time; something to do with being twins Laura assumed, telepathy perhaps.

She finished making the lunch, put it on the kitchen table and called the boys in. They were looking a lot better; the colour had returned to their cheeks, and Laura, feeling their heads, realised that their temperatures had dropped.

'Back to playgroup for you two tomorrow,' she told them.

Jack and George looked delighted and scrambled on to their chairs to eat their lunch. The twins were only ever truly quiet when they were eating, so Laura grabbed the chance to use the phone. The girls were having a night out and she had been invited. The phone was in the hall and she sat on the stairs to use it.

She could see the boys from this position, and smiled to herself as she watched them peering into their sandwiches to make doubly sure they contained something they liked. First Laura dialled the babysitter, Jane. The girl's brother answered and rock music could be heard in the background.

'Hello, James, it's Laura. Is Jane there?'

'I'll get her – who is it?' came the reply.

'It's Laura Peters.'

James held the phone in the crook of his neck and called to his sister, 'Jane, Jane! It's the phone for you. The one with the twins! Well, I don't know what she wants, do I? Come here and find out.'

A door in another part of the house slammed, dulling the music slightly, Jane picked up the extension in her mother's bedroom.

'Hello?'

'Hello, Jane, it's Laura. The boys are a lot better. Do you think perhaps you could babysit tonight after all? I haven't left it too late, have I?'

'No, not at all,' lied Jane. She would have to cancel a date with her boyfriend now; he wouldn't be pleased, but she needed the money. 'What time do you need me?' she asked.

'Would seven thirty be okay? I should have them in bed by then. I'll probably be meeting the others at about eight, I don't know where yet, but I'll leave the phone number next to the phone in case of emergencies...'

'No need to worry, Laura,' said Jane, raising her eyes to the ceiling. 'I'm sure they will be perfectly okay with me. You go out and enjoy yourself you deserve it!'

'Okay,' said Laura, instinctively looking towards the kitchen to check that the boys were all right. 'I suppose I do, I can't remember the last time I went out... see you tonight, then. Bye.'

She put down the receiver and dialled Paula. Paula was her oldest friend. They had known each other since junior school, and Paula had been there to help her all through the trauma of losing Jez. She held her hand when the twins were born by Caesarian section, and laughed and cried with her at the joy of holding them in their arms for the first time. She had even helped to wash and weigh them, wrapping them both gently like two precious stones in the green cotton sheets the midwife had given her to keep their bodies warm. She had practically taken over in theatre and had, all the staff agreed, been a wonderful help.

The phone rang and the call waiting system beeped through into Laura's ear. She held on to the phone. Come on Paula, answer the phone, tell them you'll phone back!

'Yes?' Paula's voice snapped through the computerised one.

Laura jumped, and replied, 'Paula, it's me. I think I will come tonight after all, but I need to know the time for the babysitter and where we're going for the phone number.'

Paula swatted a fly that had been getting on her nerves all day and had finally landed on the wall next to the phone in her kitchen.

'Gotcha, you little bastard!' she screamed.

'Where the hell's that?' hollered Laura. 'Have we been there before?'

'What? Very funny, no, I've just squashed a fly that's been bugging me! We're going to the new wine bar that's opened in the High Street, apparently it's quite good. I've cut the coupon out of the local paper, which gives us a twenty per cent discount on food and a free bottle of the house plonk. Should be a good evening!'

Laura agreed to meet her there at about eight.

*

The babysitter arrived late. The boys sensing that something was going on, refused to go to bed, preferring instead to hang around their mother's bedroom door and get in the way. Laura was laying out clothes on her bed.

'Where are you going, Mummy?' Jack asked picking up a bra and examining it closely.

'Out!' said Laura, gently taking the bra away from him again and laying it back on the bed above her knickers.

'Out where?' queried Jack picking up a pop sock.

'None of your business, Mr Nosey!' she teased taking back the pop sock and putting it on to the clothes horse she was creating on the bed.

Laura called down the stairs to the babysitter who was busy picking up toys and throwing them back into the toy chest.

Jane came up the stairs and took control. Tucking a twin under each arm, she horse galloped to their room reducing the boys to squeals of delight. Laura shut her door and looked at the mirror image of herself that she had created on the bed. Blue jeans, crisp white shirt, black pop socks and smart shoes.

'Yep, that will do,' she said to herself and proceeded to get dressed.

*

The wine bar was unusually busy for a Thursday night. Groups of people, mostly businessmen unwinding after a hard day at their offices, stood around the bars drinking or eyeing up the women, who were mostly propped up on stools and huddled round small oak tables within the room. The wine bar had a Western theme and Laura could see her friends in a far corner being asked for their drinks order by a waitress in full cowgirl costume, holding a tray that was shaped like a cowboy's lasso.

The girls spotted Laura and waved to her enthusiastically. They had already had a drink and were in an excitable mood. Laura squeezed through the people in the bar and over to her table. Paula stood up to greet her; sitting next to her were Sharon and Rebecca, giggling over a magazine article they were holding between them.

'About bloody time you got here!' said Paula, holding out her cheek for a kiss. 'These two have done nothing but drive me crazy over a competition in this week's magazine,' she explained.

Laura sat down next to Paula and hung her jacket on the back of a chair.

'Why, what do you win?' she enquired, tucking her long brown hair behind her ears and stretching across the table for a better look.

'What do you *win*?' shouted Sharon in disbelief.

'What do you win?' Laura repeated.

'You only win a date with Nicky Silver and a make-over, that's all,' said Sharon, a little too sarcastically for Laura's taste.

'Nicky Silver, the pop star?' said Laura, her voice trembling.

'No, Nicky Silver, the road sweeper,' said Rebecca, taking a swig of her Bacardi and coke.

'All right, everyone, calm down!' said Paula, grabbing a handful of peanuts and popping them into her mouth one at a time.

Laura was excited. Nicky Silver and the Hair Razors were one of the biggest bands of all time. Everyone loved them and to have the opportunity to actually go out with one of them – not just one of the band, but the lead singer Nicky – was an opportunity too good to miss. Laura read out the rules.

'State in not more than twenty words why you would like a date with Nicky Silver—'

'Because he's got a big dick!' said Rebecca, a little too loudly. Half the wine bar immediately went quiet. This was followed by screeches of laughter.

'Don't be childish,' said Laura, continuing to peer at the rules and the photo of her idol.

'What else have you got to do?' said Paula.

'You've got to send in a photo of yourself,' said Laura, looking at Paula for an answer.

'What for?' said Paula.

'Because he doesn't want to spend the evening with an old dog, of course,' said Sharon.

'That rules you out, then,' said Rebecca, beginning to tire of the whole discussion.

The waitress returned to the table to take their food orders.

Paula got the discount voucher she had cut from the local paper out of her bag and showed it to the waitress.

'We've got this voucher that entitles us to twenty per cent off and a bottle of wine,' she said.

The waitress took the voucher from her and scrutinised it.

'This only entitles you to twenty per cent off your food, not theirs,' she said, nodding in the direction of the other girls.

'What do you mean?' said Paula, taking the voucher back and looking at it again.

'I mean it only entitles you to a discount, not your friends,' she repeated.

'What are you talking about?' argued Paula, getting irritated. 'It says twenty per cent off food, it doesn't say twenty per cent off one portion.'

'I'll have to go and get the manageress,' the waitress whined, turning on her spurs and heading towards the bar area.

'Bloody cheek!' said Sharon.

'We had better get the free bottle of wine,' whined Rebecca, and Sharon agreed.

Laura wasn't listening. Everything around her had become a blur; all she could see was the magazine article and the photograph of Nicky Silver. She had been a fan of his for years and now had the chance to meet him. She wanted to win the competition, badly, but she never won competitions; she had entered loads of them and the nearest she had ever come to success was when she had won an apron for writing a limerick. This one was different; she had to win this one. She needed it, wanted it, and was prepared to think hard about how to win it.

The waitress returned with the manageress in tow. She was a beautiful young girl and, Paula deduced, couldn't be more than twenty-two. As if to prove that she was in charge, she wore the outfit of a Cherokee Indian with a large feather head-dress in all the colours of the rainbow, her long shiny blonde hair looking peculiarly out of place beneath it. Paula wasn't going to let her beautiful good looks, shiny blonde hair and perfect nose intimidate her, and she opened her mouth ready to let rip about the authenticity of her voucher.

But the Indian got there first.

'I understand you have got a complaint regarding our opening offer,' she said, in the squeakiest little voice the girls had ever heard.

Laura collapsed with the giggles. Retrieving her jacket from the back of her chair she began to chew it in earnest while at the same time pretending to examine one of its blue buttons.

Paula was in her element. Beautiful maybe, but with that voice most definitely a bimbo. Probably slept her way into the job, she deduced. Excellent!

'That's right,' she said, 'we have. This voucher says twenty per cent off food and a bottle of wine. It does not say anything about us only being entitled to money off one portion, there are four of us here and we want twenty per cent off the whole bill or there will be trouble.'

Laura wondered what sort of trouble that might be, and stopped chewing her button immediately. Scared stiff, she glared at Paula.

Paula ignored her. The manageress burst into tears and explained that she was only doing her job and that she 'really couldn't be held responsible for the actions of upper management.' She told the girls that they could choose anything they wanted from the menu at a twenty per cent discount, and in a final desperate squeak she told them that they could choose any wine they wanted because she was 'utterly utterly pissed off with the job already.' The girls chose the most expensive bottle of claret and got drunk.

With the food eaten, the claret polished off and the bill paid, the girls drifted out into the cold night air. Autumn had slowly turned into winter. Small flakes of snow were showering down on to the pavements and making a dusting of white on the roofs of the shops and the windscreens of cars parked precariously in the side streets.

Paula hailed a cab and the girls piled in. Rebecca and Sharon proceeded to open a window and hurl drunken comments out of it towards the unsuspecting public who were strolling ambling or rushing towards their destinations.

'Have you got a licence for that thing?' Sharon screeched as she spotted a woman in a fur coat.

'Give us a snog!' shouted Rebecca to a passing workman.

'Piss off!' he yelled back.

Laura once again wasn't listening. She opened the rolled up magazine she had clutched in her hand and gazed once more into the smiling face of Nicky Silver.

She read the competition rules through again: 'State in not more than twenty words why you would like a date with Nicky Silver.' This would need some serious thinking about, Laura concluded as the taxi rolled to a halt outside her house.

Sharon and Rebecca were by now in a semi-conscious state from the booze and only half heard Laura's friendly goodbyes. Paula had sobered up and was looking at her old friend.

'Did you enjoy yourself tonight?' she asked, her fondness for Laura and sympathy for her loss of Jez showing in her turquoise blue eyes.

Laura kissed her friend's cheek and squeezed her shoulder in reassurance.

'I've got the boys,' she reminded her. 'I haven't got time to feel sorry for myself.'

The taxi glided away and Laura stood on the path outside her house for a few minutes watching its yellow light fade into a blur before turning to let herself in through the front door. The house was a total mess. Toys, teddys and building blocks lay scattered all over the hall and down the stairs. The babysitter was asleep. Curled in a ball on the settee, she looked peaceful and childlike, much younger than her seventeen years, and vulnerable. Laura decided to call her a taxi.

Once again she waved goodbye to a fading yellow light and returned to the serenity of her home. Putting the toys away could wait until tomorrow. Laura switched off the hall light and climbed the stairs to the landing. She peeked into the boys' room. Shivering, she pulled the boys' duvets over their shoulders and kissed them both lightly goodnight. Returning to her own bedroom she laid out the magazine and started to write on its application form.

> I would like a date with Nicky Silver
> because *His eyes are blue, his hair is blond*
> *and with him beside me I would like to abscond.*

Chuckling to herself she put the magazine on the floor beside her bed and went to sleep.

★

A lone beam of sunlight shone through a crack in Laura's curtains indicating the arrival of a new dawn.

She opened her eyes and glanced around her bedroom. The children were not about. She listened. All was quiet. This, she realised, was one of those rare mornings when she had awoken before them. She tiptoed over to the window and pulled the curtains apart. The snow was thicker now and had fallen through the night. Winter sunlight spread across the room like a stone thrown into a pond. It rippled through to her bed where she ran shivering from the cold.

The magazine was on the floor where she had left it and she picked it up and reread her slogan. In the cold light of day she wondered if it was quite as funny as she'd thought last night. She grimaced at its absurdity: a date with a pop star she'd secretly loved for years. Oh, what the hell, she never won competitions anyway, she would send it off today. She propped her head up on her pillow and turned on the radio. Music drifted across the room and mingled with the rays of the winter sun, and Laura relaxed. Then the twins came bounding into the room and jumped on her bed, and that was that.

Laura fed them, clothed them and took them both to plays school. The double buggy was hard to push through the snow, but the main roads had been cleared, the fluffy white snow turned to mush by the volume of foot traffic that had passed before them. It was Friday and Laura needed to rush in order to get to the post office to buy a stamp, to post the letter that was to change her destiny.

She then needed to get back home to do some serious housework before the arrival of the weekend and the onslaught of the children and her children's friends who would call round to play, screeching with delight with every move they made and every toy they played with.

Laura smiled as she thought of it. Why did she tidy the house only to have it messed up again? For the same reason as everyone else, she deduced: routine, cleanliness, something to do.

*

Nicky Silver was at a wedding at the city zoo and he was hating every minute of it. The snow was lying six inches high on the grassy perimeters of the animals' enclosures, but the paths that surrounded them leading to the function halls had fortunately been swept clear by the keepers. The weather was awful, even for that time of the year, and the revellers at the wedding had stayed determinedly within the shelter of the deep red and gilt ballroom where the festivities were taking place. All except Nicky, who had pulled on his huge duffel coat and taken himself out of the confines of the room's finery to the cool crisp atmosphere outside.

He took the path to the monkey enclosures and visited the gorillas. Sasha, a big female, was sitting at the back of her enclosure picking her nose and examining a bogey. Her mate, a younger, fitter silverback, was pacing up and down the enclosure like a man possessed. The keeper had been in to give them lunch and had left a huge dishful of bananas and oranges but forgotten the grapes, and the silverback had the hump. He liked grapes, especially at lunchtime.

He knew there was a big wedding party on, though, and that there would be a lot of fruit left over from that; but he probably wouldn't get any until the day after tomorrow and then it would be going soft. He glanced over at the wife still sitting in the corner like a big lump. Always satisfied with a bogey, that one, he thought to himself. Her neck was no doubt covered in fleas by now, but even the thought of eating those couldn't compensate for the fact that there were no grapes on the menu today. The large gorilla swung his arms from side to side and he continued to pace up and down the enclosure protected from the public by reinforced glass. Who the bloody hell's this now? he thought, as he saw Nicky Silver press his famous face against the glass. With one swift manoeuvre he punched the glass in front of Nicky's nose, sending the star reeling back from the shock.

Momentary shock turned to surprised laughter for the star as he fell backwards on to the wooden slats of a viewing bench and shook his fist at the aggravated primate. Guy had slumped off to the corner of his living quarters clutching a banana, and he shook his fist back at Nicky.

Nicky took out the photo of Laura and looked into her smiling face for the third time that day.

He knew already that he loved her. He could tell from her smile and from the way it creased into two dimples on her pretty cheeks. He knew from the slight twinkle he could see in her eyes that she had a sense of humour and a sense of fun that he had not managed to find in any woman before. He knew he loved her when he looked at the curly brown hair that framed her face, making her look both sexy and stunning. God he wanted her, he wanted her now, but he was going to have to wait for the dinner date. Its absurdity became more apparent to him as he looked at Laura's face and he remembered how his manager had told him that he had wanted to organise a date with a fan for publicity and promotion of the band.

Publicity and promotion! Sod that, he thought to himself. I need a woman to settle down with, a wife who can look after me – someone I can look after and share my life with. 'Things are looking good and I need someone to share it all with!' He said the last bit out loud, and to Guy. Guy glared back, shuffled his position and turned his back on him; then he got mad again and beat his chest menacingly at Nicky, who got the message and moved from the viewing benches preferring to sit opposite some monkeys instead. The monkeys swung from branch to branch by their tails and ignored him.

The thick glass doors of the enclosure swung open, allowing a gust of cold air to enter the privacy of Nicky's thoughts. Terry, Nicky's manager, strode up to him and patted the star's tired shoulders with one huge hand.

'Been looking everywhere for you, Nick,' he said, easing his giant frame on to the bench beside him.

Nicky tried to hide the photo of Laura but it was too late. Terry had clocked it and was grinning at him now, enjoying watching him squirm. He noticed a flush rise into the younger man's cheeks.

'You like the look of this girl, don't you, Nick?'

Nicky wrapped his coat harder around him.

'You've let a draught in, Terry.'

'Don't change the subject,' said Terry, taking the photo from him.

'You like this girl, don't you?'

'All right then, yes I do! I fancy her like mad.'

Terry got up and studied the monkeys behind the glass.

'Look, Nicky, like the girl by all means, but try and remember this is just a publicity stunt.' He turned to face his star – 'You take the kid out to dinner, I tip off the papers and we get a few photos taken. The story goes into the press, your tour gets more publicity, the money comes rolling in and the girl goes home happy: she's met her idol and she tells all her friends about it, that's it, end of story!'

Nicky glared at him.

'No, this one's different, Tel, I can see from her photo that this one's going to be special, I want this date to go really well, I want to impress her...' he said.

'Impress her!' said Terry, his mood turning to irritation. 'You've already *impressed* her with your music.'

Nicky cut him short. 'Let's get back to the party,' he said.

'There's no arguing with you in this mood,' said Terry, and laughed. The pair left the animals and went back to the party.

*

Laura was sitting at her kitchen table with Paula and she was excited. The letter from Nicky Silver's promotion team had arrived and the girls were examining it from top to bottom.

'You lucky cow!' exclaimed Paula for the third time that morning.

'I can't believe it!' said Laura, giggling. 'Me on a date with Nicky Silver! What am I going to wear? Who's going to look after the twins? I'm never going to get over this, Paula – a date with Nicky Silver, and it's all for me!'

Paula looked at her old friend and laughed. She had never seen Laura so happy and she noticed a bloom in her cheeks only attainable by a woman who was totally in love with someone. It was a look she had not seen in her friend since her wedding six years ago. God, was it really six years since she'd married Jez? A shadow crossed Paula's face. She still hurt when she thought of Jez and how much he had loved Laura. The accident should never have happened. But, and she chastised herself for such a thought, it did, and now her old friend seemed happy for the first time in years, truly happy.

'Don't worry about what to wear,' she said to her friend. 'You always look gorgeous, whatever you wear. Anyway it says here in the letter that your prize includes two hundred pounds for a new outfit. *Two hundred pounds*! You can go up West with that lot and get yourself something stunning to wear!'

The girls looked at each other and screeched with delight.

'Hooray, hooray hooray hooray!' they sang as they danced around the kitchen table.

The date was set for a month's time. Laura had received her cheque and had spent a marvellous day in London choosing a new dress. She had gone for a black one and had been surprised that two hundred pounds didn't go as far as she had thought it might. She'd had to buy the shoes herself, something she would have been proud to do, but Paula had a whinge about it.

'They should pay for the shoes as well,' she had said.

'They probably think they are,' Laura had said and laughed, clutching her carrier bag full of new dress close to her. 'If it wasn't for you making me spend the whole lot on this one dress I could have afforded a pair of cheap shoes, at least.'

'Rubbish!' said Paula as they had climbed on to the bus home. 'Cheap shoes look cheap, that's my philosophy!'

Nothing could dampen Laura's spirits, not even the rain that had started to fall on the City, accentuating the greys of St Paul's Cathedral and leaving damp pools around the bus stops and at the feet of the people who stood at them, comforting themselves with their own thoughts and carrier bags. None of them, thought Laura, had a secret like hers.

None of them was going to go on a date with the delightful Nicky Silver.

*

Two days before the date Laura began to panic. She phoned Paula.

'What if he doesn't like me?' she asked.

'He'll like you,' said Paula.

'He might not, he might think I'm frumpy.'

'Frumpy? In that dress! You must be joking, you'll knock him dead in it! Anyway, he should think himself lucky to be going out with you.'

'Why is he lucky to be going out with me? He's the superstar – he can go out with anyone he likes: top models, actresses, anyone!'

Laura could feel the panic rising inside her leaping out of her mouth in a final crescendo of pure unadulterated fear at the thought of meeting someone so famous.

'Calm down!' yelled Paula.

'What time are they picking you up?' she asked.

'A car's coming to get me at six on Friday and then taking me to the restaurant to meet him. I'm going to have some photos taken with him first, and then the dinner.'

'How do you know you're having photos?' Paula wanted to know.

'Someone phoned me from the record company and told me. They said they would arrange it all at their end and that someone would be in the car to come with me, thank God! I don't think I could cope on my own with just the chauffeur. I'd be a nervous wreck!'

'A chauffeur?' cried Paula. 'You lucky cow!'

'Stop being so jealous. Are you still okay to babysit for me?'

'Yes, of course I am. I'll be there Friday five o'clock. Now stop worrying about the boys, they'll be fine.'

She hung up. Always worrying, she thought. Why can't she just be pleased for herself?

But Laura was pleased for herself. She was pleased beyond compare. She couldn't wait for her special evening, she couldn't wait to meet him and talk to him and tell him how much she had enjoyed his music over the years. And she wanted to tell him about her life, how unhappy she'd been on her own, and how if it hadn't have been for the boys that she might not have been able to get through it all, or cope without a man to be strong in her life, to lead her through its ups and downs and complexities.

But most of all she just wanted to be near him.

Friday night arrived very quickly. Laura tried to muddle through the day and follow her same routine. She took the boys to play school and threw all their toys into the toybox, not in anger but with a new found enthusiasm for an old chore.

She tidied the house from top to bottom. She didn't know why, and she hung and rehung her new dress up on the outside of her wardrobe in order to stare at it and to imagine herself in it. She wanted to try it on again but the housework had left her a bit sweaty so she didn't dare. Instead she decided to have an early bath to prepare for the evening ahead. There would be no chance for it once the children got home.

*

Nicky Silver was sitting in a coffee bar in Covent Garden going over the final details for the date with his manager. Terry was slurping cappuccino from a tiny cup which looked hideously quaint in his large, rugged hands.

'Are you sure you've booked the table in the corner?' Nicky was saying.

Terry put down his cup and wiped some froth from his top lip with a serviette.

'The table's booked, the flowers are ordered and the photographer is booked. All you've got to remember is to turn up, look good, smile a lot and be charming! We need this kid to give a good story to the press about what a gent you are and how much she's enjoyed herself...'

Nicky was ignoring most of what he said. He wasn't interested in what the bloody press thought about it. He just wanted her to have a lovely evening, to enjoy herself and to be pampered in a way that he knew would please her.

He ordered another cappuccino and turned to Terry.

'I think I'm in love with her, Terry,' he said.

Terry almost choked on Nicky's words.

'*In love* with her?' he spluttered. 'You don't even know the girl!'

'I don't need to have met her already to know her,' Nicky told him quietly. 'I can see from her photo that she is beautiful and I can tell from her caption that she's got a sense of humour. What else is there to know?'

'Plenty!' said Terry waving away a third cup of coffee. 'Like she might have some funny habits.'

'Funny habits! What sort of funny habits, you idiot?'

'Well, I don't know, do I, she just might that's all,' blustered Terry.

'And then again she might not – she might be the lovely person that I believe her to be, and whether you like it or not I'm bloody well going to find out tonight!' retorted Nicky.

*

Laura had stepped out of her bath and was drying her hair, naked, oblivious to the conversation taking place about her in another part of London. She had calmed down a bit and was looking at herself in the mirror as she dried her long brown hair. The curls were kicking in and framed her face beautifully; she was not having a bad hair day and was pleased about that. Everything was going well and she had an hour to kill before she picked the boys up. She finished drying her hair and started to paint her nails, plying the white polish on thickly.

She picked the children up and walked slowly home. Some of the other mothers knew about her date and wished her well with it. The rest of the day seemed to fly by; with the children to keep her company, she barely had the time to think about what the evening had in store for her. Instead, she got on with her usual work and kept one eye on the kitchen clock, waiting for its hands to strike five and for Paula to arrive to take over with the boys and give her some much needed reassurance.

The doorbell made her jump, and she glanced at the clock. It was Paula.

Paula fussed about her like a mother hen for the next hour. She gave the children some sweets and played them a new video to keep them happy, while she helped Laura into her dress and applied her make-up for her. The doorbell rang again at exactly six and a stretched black limo was waiting outside.

Some of the neighbours had come out to gawp at the scene, while others looked from behind their twitching net curtains. Laura was ready; a sort of calm enveloped her as she made her way down the stairs and out into the crisp night air. The boys ran out with Paula to wave her off and before she knew where she was, she was being whisked through the streets of London and on to her destination.

As promised she was accompanied in the car by a representative of Nicky Silver's record company, who explained to Laura that some photographers would be outside the restaurant to take pictures and that a reporter would be asking her some questions about the date afterwards.

Laura was finding it all very exciting but was secretly hoping that she would have some time on her own with Nicky.

The girl from the record company sat beside her and smoothed out the creases in her raw silk suit.

'Are you excited?' she asked Laura.

Laura jumped. 'Yes, but worried, too,' she said.

'Worried?' said the girl from the record company. 'You've got nothing to be worried about. Nicky will look after you.'

'What's he like?' asked Laura, as she checked her face for the umpteenth time in her mirror.

The girl laughed. 'Oh, Nicky's lovely,' she said, 'a real gentleman! You are going to have a super evening, don't worry about that. Look, we're here.'

The limo drew up outside the restaurant. Its exterior was painted a bottle green and brass lamps overhung its windows subtly illuminating its beauty. As she'd been told, photographers were waiting for her and their flashes momentarily blinded her as she climbed out of the car and was guided through the restaurant doors.

Nicky Silver, her idol, her love was standing by a table waiting for her. The table was dressed in a pink tablecloth and crystal glasses sparkled on it, made more beautiful by the flickering of a lone candle. Laid at her place was a singular red rose and beside this stood a pile of CDs of every record Nicky had ever made. Nicky held out his arms to Laura and she forgot all her fears and misgivings about him and herself and the date and ran into his arms. They looked into each other's eyes and they knew, they both knew that they had found each other and that nothing was ever going to separate them.

Nicky held her tight and took in the softness of her skin and the warmth of her perfumed body and realised that he had found the love he had been looking for. Laura closed her eyes and imagined herself at an old house in the country with him and her children.

The green of its rolling lawns appeared before her eyelids and she was there with Nicky and her boys. Nicky's arms were outstretched and he was playing aeroplanes with them. Laura was sitting on the swing that hung from the old oak and she was laughing. Really laughing.